Love Hawaii Time

A Mystical Love Story

Genie Joseph, MFA, PhD.

Eve Publishing

Published by Eve Publishing
R.R. 5, Rockwood, ON N0B 2K0 Canada
www.evepublishing.com

Cover: "The Mana Keepers" by Kristin Zambucka

Hawaiian Quilt Patterns Designed by John Serrao
http://www.poakalani.net/resources.html

This is a work of fiction. Names, characters, incidents and places, (other than well known cities in Hawaii and New York) are the products of the author's imagination or are used fictitiously.

First Edition 2013

Second Edition 2015

ISBN 978-0-9919798-0-6

What others are saying about Love Hawaii Time

"I loved this book and couldn't put it down. It's a feel-good book that makes you think about how best to live your life."

T.J. Covington, US Army Veteran

"So many relationship arguments are really about the different ways we relate to time. **Love Hawaii Time** explains how we each have our unique ways of 'being in time' and how we can love each other's natural ways."

Jon Terrell, MA, psychotherapist

"**Love Hawaii Time** helps you include the spirit world as a partner in love. Sometimes we need help from our ancestors to make the best choices."

Chris Miller, MA, Non-Violent Communication Trainer

"**Love Hawaii Time** is a mystical love story that helps you navigate the mysteries of love."

Howard Reyes, MSW, LCSW

*"**Love Hawaii Time** shows you not only the magic of love in Hawaii, but how you can work with that magic wherever you are in the world."*

Matthew Gray, Hawaii Food Tours
and former co-host of Love Life Radio

"Every time I picked up Genie Joseph's Love Hawaii Time I was transported back to the "island paradise." She takes the reader into a deeper experience of the Hawaiian culture and way of living than most tourists ever discover. It's a world of intimate relationship with nature, where all life forms – animal, vegetable and mineral - reflect back to us our inherent connection with divine source. With humor, romance and passion, the author draws us into an enlightened approach to life that can be practiced anywhere and anytime."
Bruce R. Jaffe, PhD

*"**Love Hawaii Time** may be my favorite love story of all time. It gives you hope that people from different worlds and cultures can come together and learn to love in each other's language."*

Winona Bice-Stephens, Ed. D

*"If you are going to read one love story this year, read **Love Hawaii Time**. The eternal struggle of artist and businessperson, man and woman, will have you ignoring the clock, and digging your toes into the sandy beach."*

Susan Lord, Wellness Consultant

Love Hawaii Time

A Mystical Love Story

Genie Joseph, MFA, PhD.

 Eve Publishing

Acknowledgments:

Mahalo to my editor, Gloria Nye, for her careful reading and helping me to tease out the best in this story.

And for all those, seen and unseen, who have supported me in this lifetime and others.

Mahalo to artist Kristin Zambucka for the cover art "The Mana Keepers."

For

My mother, Joanne, a poet,

who gave me life and a love of words.

And some good advice about using more commas.

Kanani O Amelika - Beauty of America

Hawaiian Quilt Pattern

Chapter One

It was three minutes later than the last time she had looked at her watch. Now he was an hour and *three* minutes late. April tried to pretend it didn't bother her as much as it did. She had rushed to make sure to be on time for this meeting and here she was, sitting in the beautiful beachside Café of the Paradise Resort, with the perfect view—and she was deleting e-mails from her phone. She was not on vacation. She had just flown ten hours on the red-eye flight from New York City to Honolulu, and she was tired.

She glanced up at the turquoise waters, white sandy beaches, lovers slowly walking arm in arm, looking into each other's eyes. That was particularly annoying. And her navy blue suit jacket felt too warm, cloying. She blew a strand of brown hair out of her eyes.

She went back to deleting e-mails. At least she got something done while she waited. April was never good at waiting. It always made her fret about something she should be doing that was more important. Waiting for someone always made her mind wander to vaguely dark places that she would rather not go.

The couple at the next table, wearing matching Aloha shirts with bright orange flowers, were feeding each other bites of pineapple. Then the man leaned over their table and sealed the moment with a slow kiss. April looked away.

She didn't have time for love. It wasn't that she'd made a conscious decision to live without it. She was just busy looking elsewhere while it slowly and imperceptibly faded to the outer edge of her reality. It had been four years since the divorce from her unfaithful husband. Just long enough to forget that something very important in her life was missing. Love just somehow slid lower and lower as a priority until it fell off her long "To Do" list. Besides, love doesn't knock on your door when your heart is still in hiding.

April's career, as an agent at Consolidated Branding, which licenses the work of talented artists' images for corporate clients, had taken over every inch of her life, and free time was a distant memory, erasing even the desire for love. Although she would never call herself a workaholic, behind her back she knew other people did. But those were just jealous co-workers, she reasoned.

While most people would kill to be sent on a business trip to Hawaii, to April this was just work. Her boss, Dana Morgan, admitted that this was why she chose April for this assignment. She knew April wouldn't treat it as a vacation, and would stay focused. Focused on the business of securing a licensing deal with Kaikoa, an emerging artist who her boss was anxious to scoop up—and add to her trophy list of creative acquisitions. April could almost cut the resentment with a knife in the conference room when her boss announced to the team that she chose April to go to Hawaii to close this deal. Even though this announcement was last minute, April knew she should feel grateful.

Dana Morgan, a retired Air Force Colonel, treated this business as if it was the most important battle of her life. She had come to Hawaii a month before to a small gallery opening, and after seeing Kaikoa's work, had attempted to make a deal with him right then and there, but he politely turned her down.

Dana had recently started an "incentive" plan which rewarded the top performer, and turned everyone into a take-no-prisoners carnivore around the office. Success was a much higher priority than camaraderie, and no one climbing to the higher rungs trusted anyone else on the same career track.

"His work is important," her boss had said.

As April looked at the slides of lush tropical flowers, with the brilliant colors, that were both natural and heightened to their ideal, they seemed to jump off the flat surface as if they were alive.

"But I must warn you. He is handsome and charming. Do not get distracted."

A jolt of energy raced up April's spine.

"I understand the mission," she assured her. "I will stay focused on the target."

She had learned that her boss responded well when she peppered her language with military jargon.

April had three days to get the contract signed, but she had a reputation for staying on task like a search and rescue dog. Her nervous system was wired for deadlines, and she actually enjoyed the structure of this kind of stress. She began mentally creating a timeline for how long it might take to review the contract with him, uncover any concerns he might have, and get revisions to NYC which is six hours ahead, and then slip back on the plane with the coveted contract signed and sealed.

She had other deals she was working on that were close to fruition, and she knew her competitive co-workers were pushing full steam ahead with theirs. April hadn't been on the island of Nature for an hour, and she was already viewing this trip as a massive interruption in her bloated schedule.

She fidgeted with the small turtle charm she wore on a gold chain around her neck. It had always brought her good luck, and she hoped it wouldn't fail her now. She was glad that at the last moment she had remembered to put it on for this trip.

A small zebra-striped grey bird landed near her table. The bird seemed to be watching April, no doubt hoping for a morsel of food, but a small sign read "Please, don't feed the birds, Mahalo."

"Sorry, birdie," April said aloud. Anyway she hadn't ordered any food yet. And she didn't think the bird would appreciate the dregs of her cappuccino. The bird stayed for several long moments, watching her, before flying away.

The waiters in the Bird of Paradise Resort restaurant had figured out she wanted to be ignored. She fidgeted restlessly, ignoring the vivid turquoise ocean view in front of her. Instead her eyes strained to review old text messages on her phone that could possibly be deleted.

She had rushed right from the airport, without showering or changing, to be on time for this appointment. With each minute ticking away she felt more irritated and sticky, and wished she had showered. There was no way she could call him to push this meeting twenty minutes later because, as her boss had already warned her, Kaikoa had no cell phone.

I could race upstairs and jump in the shower. She was an expert at fast showers, and with riding up and down the elevator to her ninth floor hotel room, she estimated she could have done it and been back down here in eighteen minutes. She could leave a note with the waiters. But if he didn't get it, and she missed him, she could lose a whole day.

Hopefully this first meeting to go over the contract she had sent ahead wouldn't take too long, especially if he had his proposed revisions written down. Then she could excuse herself to go over his notes in her room—and could take a long, luxurious shower. She would suggest they meet again for lunch to go over whatever revisions he might have. It was a good plan. But then again, she knew dealing with artists and her "good plans" didn't always match.

Thinking about having a shower made her skin feel prickly. She hadn't even laid eyes on Kaikoa and she was already annoyed by him. She was imagining some lame "artist excuse" about being drawn by the muse and losing his sense of time, and how sorry he was to have kept her waiting. She was practicing increasingly rude replies to his apology when suddenly something made her look up from her text messages. He was standing there, watching her.

His dark brown eyes locked her in his gaze. His wet, long dark hair dripped on his faded blue T shirt. The photo her boss had sent to her cell phone did nothing to convey his pure animal magnetism. He didn't utter an excuse or apology. He just stared at her in a silent greeting. His gaze settled on the turtle around her neck.

"Nice necklace."

Still startled by his silent approach, her fingers nervously fidgeted with the turtle. It took her brain several moments to unfreeze and find her words.

"How long have you been watching me?"

"Not long enough to memorize your beauty."

"Very charming line for a man who is one hour late."

"Actually I was an hour early," Kaikoa's mouth formed a slow lethal grin, "but the waves were going off." He gestured toward the ocean in front of them as if that explained everything. He sat down next to her. He was wearing surfer board shorts. His shirt clung to his still wet body.

"You look like you just stepped out of a shower."

"You look like you haven't had one yet."

April wiped the sweat off her cheek with the back of her hand, wishing he hadn't noticed.

He handed her one of the restaurant's pink linen napkins.

There was no question about it. He was beautiful. Not like magazine cover air-brushed beauty, but raw and real. His bronzed skin and high cheek bones enhanced his eyes. His thick hair fell in long dark waves. His arms were strong, and toned. There was no excess on his body, like one who spent most of his day in motion. April found herself wondering if he had been in a shower with someone just moments ago. She pushed the image from her mind, and reached inside her leather i-pod case and pulled out one of her business cards.

He didn't glance at it.

"I know who you are. Ms. April Walton, Assistant Director of Acquisitions."

On his lips, her title sounded pompous. Should she be

offended?

"Yes, we have Google in Hawaii, Ms. Walton."

"But how did you know it was me sitting here?"

"You're the only one wearing a suit."

It was true. Everyone else in the restaurant was in their island wear. Bare limbs, sandals, colorful dresses and aloha shirts were the rule.

He wasn't wearing a watch. And there wasn't a pocket for a cell phone, even if he owned one.

"You're mad at me for being late."

"I take pride in being on time. It's hard to be patient when people don't keep their time commitments."

"You love your schedule."

Was he teasing her? It was a sharp observation that came in too close, too accurate for a first meeting. She tried to contain her reaction.

"I just think people ought to respect each other's time."

"I have total respect for time," he explained patiently. "I just have a different relationship to time than you do."

"The last time I checked, we all have the same twenty-four hours in a day."

"We all have different relationships to time, because we all have different things we value."

"You are what you make of your time," April said. Why was she quoting her boss, when she absolutely hated that saying?

"I do agree," he said, "Good saying." He relaxed into the cushioned rattan arm chair across from her.

April restrained herself from saying it was her totally-driven boss's favorite saying and if she heard it one more time, she might go postal. He was, after all, a prospective client. She

7

knew better than to let her frustration spill.

"I'm sure you had a good reason for being late," she offered, with a fake smile.

"Very good reason. I don't choose to be run by schedules and man-made agreements."

"Guess not *woman*-made either."

"Yes." His voice was unperturbed by her thinly disguised irritation. "Like my ancestors, I follow the rhythm of the sun and the moon, and the waves and the wind."

"I see," April said, not bothering to be more diplomatic. She was still angry about not being able to take a shower and then having been made to wait over an hour for the honor of his presence.

"I hope you will see," he said.

"What exactly is it you want me to see?"

"I want you to see that we don't all have the *same* 24 hours."

"Does your watch, if you wore one, have 26 hours?"

"I make different choices about how I relate to time, because I have a different relationship to time."

April couldn't resist interrupting with "Well, if you respected time...."

"I have complete respect," he said calmly, *"For Hawaii Time."*

April knew this conversation wasn't going anywhere near her objective. She decided to redirect it to the business she had come to conduct.

"My boss, Colonel Dana Morgan—"

"Retired Colonel," he corrected.

"Yes. Retired. I know she has been in conversations with you about your art work. She was supposed to come for

8

this meeting, but three days ago she got a sinus infection and the doctors wouldn't let her fly.

"Lucky for you."

April looked away from his penetrating eyes. If there were any other meanings hidden in those words, she didn't want to appear curious. She tried to redirect her mind back to business.

"She briefed me on the terms of the..."

"Then she must have told you."

"What? Told me what?"

"That I turned her down."

April's face couldn't hide the fact that this was news to her.

Just as she was mustering a reply, a pretty waitress in a colorful curve-hugging muumuu, approached with a plate of food. She placed the plate of eggs, sausages and white rice before him, fawning as if he were royalty. April had always thought muumuus were big and baggy, but this one was tightly fitted around all the dangerous curves.

"I brought your favorite," the waitress said, with that subtle hint of familiarity in her body language that most men miss and most women don't. "And of course a large glass of POG."

April wanted to know what POG was. It looked inviting, but she didn't feel like asking a question that would brand her as an outsider.

Kaikoa noticed she was staring at the tall, cool pink drink.

"Are you eating?" Kaikoa asked. She could see he was a little uncomfortable with all the gushing attention *he* was getting.

"I got upgraded to first class, they feed you every half-hour."

"Bring her a fruit plate," he said.

"Oh, yes. That sounds perfect. Here I am in Hawaii. Duh."

"Would you care for another cappuccino?" The waitress asked, turning to April as if an afterthought.

"Two is enough," Kaikoa answered for her.

The waitress removed the empty coffee cup, and flashed one more smile to Kaikoa as she left. April restrained herself from asking if this smiling lady was a special friend of his.

"How did you know it was my second cup?"

"Two empty packets of brown sugar."

She looked over at the packets. "You're very observant. I guess that is one of the qualities that makes you such an exquisite artist."

He ignored her compliment, and she made a mental note that this strategy, which was usually so effective with other artists, was not working with Kaikoa.

"And how do you know that two is enough?"

"You're already wound tightly enough. We want to take you in the other direction. Try this." He moved his glass of pink juice toward her. It looked quite refreshing.

"I couldn't drink anything with the name POG."

"POG is passion juice mixed with orange and guava juice. If you don't like it, feel free to spit it out on me."

April smiled. He hadn't earned a genuine smile yet, but she took a small sip. It was cool and refreshing. She drank half the glass in one swallow. She could have done it in one, but he was watching her, and she didn't want to give him the

10

satisfaction.

"Eat your eggs," she said.

He descended on his plate of French toast with eggs sunny-side up, sausage, and white rice. He had surprisingly good table manners, using his silverware in the European style, holding the fork pointed down in the left hand and using the knife with the right. He gave his food his whole attention, chewing carefully. She wondered if he had gone to boarding school abroad. She was glad his attention was elsewhere so she could gather her thoughts.

April caught herself staring. She pulled hard on the reigns in her brain, and reminded herself: *This is a very important business meeting. I have a job to get done.* Especially since her boss had not succeeded, it would be a real feather in April's cap to reel him in and get this deal signed, sealed and delivered. She ran through her three day plan. "*I can do this,*" she said again to herself.

Perhaps it was the ten-hour flight, because she found her mind wandering away from her attempts at controlling her thoughts. His strong arms and shoulders were a total distraction. But it was his eyes that were dangerous. Smoky, smoldering, sensuous. And full lips, now shiny with egg. His tongue massaged them away.

"We Fed-Ex'd the contract last week. I assume you've read it."

He shook his head 'no.'

"Oh." April began scrolling on her phone. "Shall I send it to you again?"

"I said we had Google in Hawaii. I didn't say I had a computer."

"Okay," she said patiently. He wasn't her first artist to

be technically challenged. "I have a hard copy in my room…"

He looked up at her.

Oh, no. Was he thinking that she meant something? "I mean, I could bring it down," she said, now wondering if he had any thoughts about coming up to her room. The more he studied her, the more she felt compelled to change the subject. But her mind wasn't working right. She fidgeted with her spoon.

"What's your cat's name?' he asked.

"What? How did you know I have a cat?"

He reached across the table and plucked a cat hair from the sleeve of her navy blue suit. She wished again that she hadn't just gone straight from the plane to this meeting without changing. But then *she* didn't want to chance being late to their first meeting.

"Angelina," she said.

"Angeleeena" he purred, as if feeling the cat's essence from the single hair that he held between his fingers. "She is a very sweet kitty. Welcome to Hawaii, Angelina." And with that he blew the strand of cat hair into the breeze and watched it float away.

"At least your cat likes Hawaii."

"I'm sure Hawaii is a very lovely place, but I am just here for three days to get this contract—"

"You're not sure at all that Hawaii is a lovely place. Your eyes aren't even open yet. You've been sitting here next to the ocean for over an hour. Have you even put your toe in the water?"

April fidgeted in her chair; her panty hose were feeling like prison for legs. Her tailored suit was perfectly appropriate for a New York meeting, but here in Hawaii she felt as if she was wearing a clown suit. It wasn't just her wardrobe that wasn't hitting the mark. She was going to have to recalibrate her entire strategy with Kaikoa. Clearly her 'get down to business' mindset was not going to fly. *Not a problem.* She prided herself on her flexibility of approach – a necessity when dealing with artists of various temperaments. She would have to slow down—just a little—to build rapport.

She looked over at the ocean. It was turquoise and peaceful, and watching the movement of the waves began to calm the molecules of her mind.

"There. See? It's nice to be touched by the place you are visiting. It's almost rude not to be," he said.

April felt herself being charmed, against her will and better judgment, of course. She remembered one of the negotiation techniques she had learned in a recent company training: when you hit a wall in one area, return to an area of common ground. She decided to talk about her cat.

"Angelina is the sweetest cat. I rescued her when she was five weeks old."

He nodded, but looked very solemn.

"Now it's her turn to rescue you."

She had no answer. It was a relief when the waitress returned with a plate of fruit and put it in front of her. *How could he know I love fresh fruit?*

"Mahalo," Kaikoa said. The waitress put a new glass of POG juice in front of him. Apparently she had watched him give April his glass.

"Would you like another glass of POG?" the waitress asked April.

April nodded, regretting giving Kaikoa the satisfaction of being right about how good it was.

"How did you know to order this for me?"

"You look like a fruity-kind of girl."

April wondered whether or not that was a good thing, but he said it with his slow smile. She had no doubt it could melt any girl within a mile radius. She turned to the fruit plate, which was arranged like a work of art, in the shape of a rainbow. She was impressed with how the chef used colors to complete the effect. The kiwi, raspberry, blackberry, mango and the fanned strawberry with a spread of mint. The marketer in her saw this image as a potential post card, and she couldn't resist taking a picture with her cell phone.

She looked up at his bemused smile.

"This flower. It's so . . ." The purple orchid in the center of the fruit rainbow had white-edged petals. It was placed between the papaya and the pineapple on her plate, bewitching her with its grace. She couldn't take her eyes off the delicate flower. "Do they put one of these on every plate?"

"That's pretty much an everyday thing around here." He seemed amused at her fascination. "But that one is completely unique," he offered.

"Why?"

"Because you have looked at it with such tenderness."

She laughed, dismissing this. Colonel Morgan had warned her about his charm. She had a sudden pang of shame that she was only here to help her company make a lot of money from branding his imagery. Of course, he would profit from the deal, and being good at her job meant keeping such feelings at bay. It would not help her in the negotiation if Kaikoa thought she was just here to make a buck off other people's creative visions. She couldn't help wondering if he thought that about her already. Or maybe it was just a passing twinge of her own self-loathing peeking through her professional mask.

"Don't you believe that flower can feel your eyes?" he asked.

"Frankly, no," she shrugged. "I mean not in the human sense of the word."

"I suppose you're the kind of girl who thinks that a relationship to a flower is a one-way admiration."

She thought about that for a moment. He had a point. Not a very logical one, but it was interesting to consider.

"I suppose you're the kind of guy who talks to flowers."

"I have been known to. Especially if I need an answer to an important question."

She looked into his eyes. They were soft and strong, and she knew she shouldn't let herself slide inside any further. "Do you have a license for those eyes?" She was immediately embarrassed that she had said that out loud.

He ignored her words which had somehow slipped out of her self control. It was never a good idea to have a first negotiation meeting when you were too tired.

"Shall I show you?" he said, tenderly picking up the flower.

"What?"

"How to talk to a flower."

"Yeah. Sure." She didn't believe any of this, but she would play along. He seemed very interested to show her.

"Think of a 'yes' or 'no' question."

"How will I get my answer?"

"We'll ask the flower to answer."

The question surged onto her mind screen before she could edit it. *'Are you and I going to be lovers?'* The words repeated in her brain. She chased it away with all her will.

This was not the question to be asking about a man she had just met—and especially one she had met on business. Definitely this question should not be allowed to slip out of her mouth. She reminded herself to keep strong control over her words, if not her thoughts. She wished she had slept better on the flight. It was certainly not the question to be wriggling its way through her mind during such an important pending business deal. One of the reasons she had been chosen for this assignment was her reputation for being sensible and business-minded, even when dealing with seductive and creative and often times narcissistic artists.

Her boss usually made two or three trips a year to Honolulu, often coinciding with First Friday. On the first Friday of the month in Chinatown, many small galleries and shops were open for the night time walking event within a several block radius. Dana had had good luck finding new artists at these events and signing them up. April remembered feeling a rush up her spine the first time her boss had showed her a couple of slides of Kaikoa's work. Even sitting in an office in New York, there was something about this self-trained artist whose water color images transported you. The way the colors melded over each other moved you out of ordinary time.

She was used to looking at the work of undiscovered artists, and they rarely had that kind of impact. His work was unique amid a torrent of images of flowers on the market. Somehow his brush slid through the line of reality and into the ephemera—in displays of color like bursts of energy. At the office an intern had said: "It's like they are alive." April agreed. There was something about these watercolors that made you stop, and breathe, and wonder. There was good

16

reason her boss wanted this contract signed. She knew he would be worth millions in licensing re-sales to her top drawer clients, especially in Asia.

Getting this contract signed was so important her boss had planned to make this trip herself, and had barely hid her disappointment that her sinus infection grounded her. Her boss rarely spoke to April this way, but before she left she looked her right in the eye and said, "He is handsome and terribly charming."

"He won't be the first undiscovered artist to try to charm me."

"April, I won't be watching you every second. I am counting on you not to fall in love with him."

Yes, she had been thoroughly warned about Kaikoa but nobody thought to warn her about her own desires.

"So what's your question?"

"I can't think of one," she lied.

The look he gave her suggested he knew she was lying. Knowing he knew made her skin bristle. She almost regretted lying, or at least lying with such transparency. If he knew she was lying, he wasn't going to grace the lie with any more words about it.

His strong brown fingers held the slender stem of the flower captive for a moment, pondering it as if it had words written inside. Then slowly he began to rotate the flower, hypnotically, as if this was a form of prayer. He dipped his other fingers in his water glass and let a few drops slide into the center of the flower. She watched this slow ritual, glad to have his focus somewhere else, so that her own eyes could wander all around him.

"Take off your jacket." She hesitated just a moment.

He watched as she slid out of her jacket.

The balmy breeze sent a wave of aliveness up her arms. She knew the pale blue silk tank top flattered her. His eyes following her newly exposed curves made the fabric feel vaguely electric.

He pushed the plates aside, clearing a path between them.

"Give me your wrist."

"What?"

She had heard him but it wasn't computing.

He demonstrated with his own arm, turning his wrist upwards, showing the light tender side.

Her brain, suddenly four-years-old, went into tantrum-freeze. *No. Don't comply. Don't do what he says. If you do, he will win.* Her mind tumbled in a spin cycle. What would she lose? It was hard to keep track of an internal argument.

His silent patience made her body comply even while her brain hadn't finished firing off objections, and she slowly offered her right wrist to him.

"Closer."

She inched her arm closer, across the great divide between them, sliding along the distance between two people who have not yet touched each other. In reality it was just a couple of inches of space between them, but in emotional terms it was a new universe. His eyes seemed to be savoring her exposed wrist. She felt primal and vulnerable, with her wrist upturned for him like a Geisha girl, presenting such a tender spot at his request.

With the deliberate grace of a tea ceremony he brought the flower just a quarter inch above her wrist and twirled it ever so slowly between his fingers. It caused a sensation she could feel, although he hadn't touched her. Yet.

"Remember your question?"

She stared back. Words were being sucked away by the flood of anticipation. How had he unleashed so many fluttery sensations? Where had they been hiding for so long?

"Yes, that one," he answered for her.

Had had he unleashed so many fluttery sensations? Where had they been hiding so long?

If he knew, he wasn't saying.

"What am I supposed to do?"

"Nothing. We just watch the water."

"I don't understand."

"The way the drop of water falls across the wrist will give us your answer."

"Which—"

"Shhh. Just watch."

He tipped the flower ever so slightly until a single drop of water rolled down the soft petal and onto her wrist. The liquid drop landed perfectly on the center of her wrist, like a homing pigeon. They both stared at the drop of water on her wrist. Then a vibration—from where?—made the water shiver, until it slowly slid down the right side of her wrist, inflaming sensations everywhere.

He watched it glide over her bare skin, entranced, until there was no trace of the liquid. His concentration added a force field as if this moment was somehow sealing their fate.

She had a million questions but the silence was too precious to disturb. He leaned back in his chair and brought the flower to his lips, brushing it against them. His eyes wandered off to the waves, lost or perhaps found in another world.

"What does it mean?" she asked, already feeling the

hunger for his attention again.

Did he hear her?   Where was his mind taking him?

He stood up, still watching the waves.

"What did it mean?" Her heart was racing for no reason, "What happened?"

"Do you see that turtle?"

"What? Where?"

"Over by the swell."

She looked out at the ocean. The same ocean he was looking at. But whatever he was seeing was not the same. To her it was just the ocean.

"I have to go talk with that Turtle."

He stood up, leaving her business card on the table where she had put it.

Wait, she wanted to say but he already leapt over the two-foot high barrier that surrounded the café.

Then he turned and flashed his magnetic smile.

"You did good," he said.

He ran toward the waves. In one smooth move he tossed his blue Tee shirt over his head, leaving it where it fell on the sand. And with the grace of one who belongs to the sea, he left her sight, and was submerged into the world of water.

Ku'uipo-Sweetheart

Chapter Two

"What do you mean you don't know how it went? Did he sign the contract?"

Her boss's voice was so loud April had to hold the phone away from her ear. She took a deep breath and told the truth.

"He hasn't read it yet."

"Didn't you overnight him?"

Dana had a way of making the most simple question sound like an inquisition and a guilty verdict in one breath.

"Yes. That doesn't mean he read it."

"I'll e-mail him another copy. What's his e-mail?"

"He doesn't have a computer." April felt her boss's irritation coming 5,000 miles through the cell phone. "Or a watch." She considered bringing up the fact that her boss had neglected to tell her he had already turned down her verbal offer, but she knew it wouldn't get her anywhere.

"Look, April, what's your game plan? I'm assuming

you have one. You know we're on a deadline here. Our portfolio goes to print in three weeks. I can't hold up the print run. Either your artist is in it—or the spot goes to Kristy. You know I want Kaikoa's plumeria on the cover, but I'm going with the first signed contract I get."

April's red-eyed, jet-lagged brain began to frazzle. Dana always used the competition between her and Kristy to get more out of both of them. She hated that it always worked.

"I know what you need. I have three days. I'll get the contract signed." April hoped her tone would be more convincing than she felt. Dana sighed on the other end. Had she been standing in front of her, Dana's eyes would be boring right into her. She could almost feel them now.

"April," she began, in the cool tone of one who enjoys putting pressure on others, "Did I send the wrong woman for this job?"

"I will get this done. And I know you like Kaikoa's work better than 'Kristy's artist.'"

"What I like is knowing that the artist I pitched to the Freeman Group is signed, sealed and delivered. What I like are signed contracts. What I like is knowing I can trust someone to get a simple job done."

"I understand." She knew when to keep her responses short.

"So, what's the next step with your artist?"

Dana's referring to Kaikoa as *her artist* took up too much RAM in her brain. She had no answer.

Her boss wasn't one to tolerate silence for long. "You had breakfast with him, I assume you gave him a hard copy of the contract. When's your next meeting?"

"He'll call me," April improvised and then remembered

that Kaikoa had left her business card on the table in the restaurant. To say nothing of the fact that she hadn't thought to bring a hard copy to breakfast.

"Alright, call me with updates every few hours. I'm sure he'll want to negotiate. Not that I don't trust you, but I may need to massage this deal."

"Right. Will do."

"And your next call better be with his deal terms. I hope you're not thinking this is a party trip to Hawaii. Got another call. Ciao."

"Ciao…" but the line was already dead.

April wanted to toss her cell phone over the hotel room balcony. She kicked herself for not bringing a copy of the contract to breakfast, but she needed to build rapport at their first meeting, not shove a twenty-eight page paper down his throat.

Now what? He wasn't carrying a cell phone, he didn't have her number. She hated to admit she had no 'next step.' Her mind saw Kristy gloating at the conference table with "her" artist in tow and his design on the cover of the company portfolio.

She headed for the shower, hoping to wash away the stress.

* * *

April loved big bathrooms. The shower in her hotel room was luxurious with its soft Hawaiian water. Nothing like the functional tiny shower in her New York City apartment. For April a good shower was like a mini-vacation, providing the perfect escape from the chatter of the mind. And the dainty sample bottles that were laid out added to the sense of everything being in order. She opened a cheerful bottle of Surrender Lavender Body Lotion and started to inhale the gentle fragrance, when the hotel room phone rang. She grabbed the plush towel and wrapped it around herself and ran to answer it.

"Were you in the shower?" It was him.

"Yes."

"That means you're nude." He made it sound nice. Like he was conjuring up this image in his mind.

"I don't generally shower in my navy blue suit."

"Put on your bathing suit and meet me on the sand."

"Um. I can't."

"Can't meet me?"

"I, uh, didn't bring a bathing suit."

"You came to Hawaii and you didn't bring a bathing suit?"

She could feel him smiling, even over the phone. "In New York City I don't have much use for one. I had one, but it is six years old and it's kind of stretched out." This was way too much information for a guy, but she couldn't stop. "I'm just not the 'go and get a bathing suit in a hurry' kind of girl. The last one took me a three-day weekend of shopping in like six stores . . ."

She suddenly wondered if he was still listening. "Hello?"

"There's a store in the lobby called Bikini Motion. Mildred will take care of you. I'll meet you on the sand. In your bathing suit."

"But I wouldn't even know where to start and it will take me hours to figure out what kind to get."

"Get one with a top and a bottom."

"Wait. I can't—"

"Yes, you can."

"When?"

"Now." His voice was sweet but firm.

"Wait, I—"

"Aloha."

"Aloha," April said to the second dial tone of the day.

*   *   *

The size-zero bikinis on the perfect-body plastic mannequins in the shop window did nothing for April's confidence. Wearing her gym shorts and a T shirt, she walked tentatively into the bikini shop in the lobby. Mildred, an octogenarian local Asian woman, the owner of Bikini Motion, seemed delighted to see her and waved her inside.

"Leilani, come here. Kaikoa picked very good one for you."

"No, I'm April—"

Mildred already had April's arm and was leading her to the fitting room.

"He did? How did he know my size?"

"He looked," Mildred said, as if this was beyond obvious.

The bikini hanging inside was irresistible—turquoise, with gold trim. It had a kind of 1940's demure styling, with a little flared skirt. Not too revealing. She was relieved. She hadn't had a bikini wax in four years.

"Mr. Kaikoa have very good taste. You try on."

Mildred ushered her inside the fitting room and closed the rickety bamboo door. April took a deep breath and began

25

undressing, but she already knew it wasn't going to fit. Nothing ever fit her right. If the top fit, the bottom made her look like somebody had squeezed a pear in the middle. If the bottom fit, the top looked like it would slip off. It just couldn't be this easy.

Or could it? The fabric was soft, and the cut was just right for her curves.

"I come in," Mildred announced and opened the door without waiting for an answer. "Yeah, yeah, perfect fit. Mr. Kaikoa, he know the ladies." Mildred giggled like a school girl. She deftly used the embroidery scissors which she wore around her neck to snip off the tags.

"Mr. Kaikoa said he pay for everything. Lucky girl."

April was too amazed at how well it fit, to object. She felt pretty and feminine. It was not too skimpy, and kind of classy. "I can't believe it fits so well. It's beautiful."

"You wear it out. Take this pareo. Everyone here wears them."

"What's a pareo?"

Mildred held a lovely matching colored piece of light flowing fabric.

"It's all we wear on the beach. You just tie the fabric around and knot it like this."

April flinched as Mildred tied a knot in the fabric tightly above her breasts.

"Don't worry, never falls down. One of Nature's miracles."

"I keep your clothes for you in a bag until you get back from the beach. You got flip flops? No?"

April looked down at her well-worn black running shoes.

"I guess size. Seven?"

"Seven and a half."

"I get for you."

She returned with a pair of perfectly fitting turquoise flip flops. "Good color for your brown hair. Leilani, you look like perfect princess now."

Mildred might not be capable of getting her name right, but April was very satisfied with her new total Waikiki look.

"How much do I owe you? I mean for the shoes and pareo."

"Mr. Kaikoa already paid." Mildred waved away her credit card. "You're in Hawaii. You go have some fun. You look like you need some fun." Mildred giggled again. When someone her age makes a joke like that, you have no choice but to laugh with her.

* * *

April walked out onto the warm, white sand. The softness giving way with each step, massaging her toes. She loved having her feet touched, but a foot massage was a luxury of time she hadn't allowed herself in years. *How long has it been since I've had one?* The fact that she couldn't remember meant it was way too long ago. She had tried to interest her ex-husband in trading foot massages, but he wasn't any good at it and never seemed willing to learn. It was just one of the many sweet things she had long ago forgotten.

A little way down the sand she saw Kaikoa talking to two pretty girls who were holding their surf boards. They had perfect trim bodies, not an ounce of fat or flab, and even from this distance she could see they were flirting with him. Her

27

confidence sank. She thought about turning around and leaving, but at that moment Kaikoa saw her and waved her over.

The girls checked April out, and left before being introduced, but not before each one reached over and gave Kaikoa a kiss on the cheek. The surfers took off down the beach and Kaikoa turned and looked at her.

"Thank you. That was an incredibly thoughtful gift," she said.

"Hey, you paid for breakfast," he said.

"I could've spent days shopping and not found anything this nice. How did you know it would fit?"

"Artist's eye."

"Do you do that for all your girls?"

"Only the girls who fly 5,000 miles first class and don't pack a bathing suit. Come on, let's go." He turned toward the water, but she didn't follow.

"You go ahead. I'll sit here on the sand and relax." April sat down defiantly on the white sand. Not used to having so little clothes on in public, she pressed her knees close to her chest. Her business suit was her uniform and she felt naked without it.

"I already spent two hours in the water this morning. We're going in for you."

"I'm not really the 'tear off your pareo in front of a guy you just met' kind of a girl."

"Okay." He sat down next to her.

"Okay?" She was surprised that he didn't try to talk her out of it.

"Were you expecting me to swoop you up in my arms and toss you in the water?"

"No. Thank you. And I'm sure you could. So, no need to prove it, King Kong."

He leaned back on his elbows to watch the waves. As they sat side by side, gazing at the turquoise ocean, she felt undefined layers slipping away. The gentle breeze, the soothing pattern of the waves, began to change the rhythm in her brain. She was settling down. No wonder they called this place Paradise.

"Is that waterproof?" he asked, pointing to her watch.

"No. I forgot I had it on. I never take it off."

"Is it an expensive watch?"

"No," she laughed, "It's one of our company's SWAG."

"What is 'swag'?"

"Stuff We All Get. Promotional stuff we give for free, like at trade shows, or for employee recognition. We sell this kind of thing to other companies to use for brand recognition. People love free stuff. I don't know why they—"

He reached over and began unfastening the watch from her arm. "You don't need it while you are here. You're on Hawaii Time"

"How will I know what time it is?"

"It's always right now."

His fingers dug into the sand, scooping out a shallow hollow. "The whole point of coming to Hawaii is to take a break and not be ruled by clock time."

"You think that just by taking off my watch you can make me forget about time?"

"It's a start. Just give yourself a few days living like this. It will rock your world."

"*My* whole point of coming to Hawaii is to negotiate a business deal with you."

He didn't respond, just continued digging, making the hole deeper. Then he placed her watch in it and covered it over with sand. She couldn't believe he was burying her watch, but couldn't think of a good enough objection to why he shouldn't.

"So you think it's just that easy to steal my time?" She had three more watches just like that one in her desk drawer in New York, but he didn't need to know that.

"I'm taking away the symbol of your old relationship to time."

"And this is important because?"

"Because I want to give you the gift of Hawaii Time."

"Is that so I can be an hour late to an important meeting because "the waves are going off?"

"That could happen."

April laughed. The energy all around her was just too warm and sweet to argue. "I would be fired on the spot. My boss is a very on-time person. She's a retired Air Force Colonel, and she expects everyone to be ten minutes early to every meeting. She fired her attorney because he was fifteen minutes late to a meeting."

"Is your boss a happy lady?"

"What? I don't know. I've never asked her."

"I've only met her once, and I can tell you she's not a happy camper."

"She's very driven, but that's why she's so successful."

"I guess it depends on how you measure success."

"I suppose you measure it by the size of the wave."

"Now that's getting personal," he teased.

She hadn't meant anything by it, but now *she* was blushing.

He stood up and held out a hand to help her up. He led

her to a more secluded section of the beach. From this angle she had a perfect view of Diamond Head, the broad, saucer-shaped crater, an iconic image of Hawaii that she had seen on so many postcards and landmark images of Paradise.

"It's really impressive in person," April said, staring in awe. "It must be a very old mountain."

"Diamond Head was formed about 300,000 years ago during an explosive eruption that sent ash and particles into the air," he explained. "When they settled, and cemented together they formed the crater."

"You can hike it, right? I read about that on the plane."

"Did you bring hiking shoes? Its 560 feet from the crater floor. Pretty vigorous hike. I'll take you if you want."

"If we have time," April said.

"Do we *have* time or *make* time?" he teased. "We always make time for the things that are most important to us."

April nodded. They walked along the edge of the water in silence for awhile. She realized she was walking ahead of him, and slowed down.

"You have someplace else you need to be?" he teased.

"Sorry. I'm just used to walking fast. In New York if you slow down, you cause a traffic jam."

"You're not in New York anymore. It's safe to slow down."

"Yeah. Wow. That feels better."

"Slow your body down to a natural rhythm, and your brain will slow down too," Kaikoa said.

They walked along in silence at a slower pace. Her brain *would* start to slow down, then it would ramp up with a stream of new thoughts. Ridiculous ones, like was he watching her butt jiggle when she walked. For some reason his capacity for silence made her feel like chattering. "I want to understand what you mean by Hawaii Time," she said.

"When the Big Game is over and the scoreboard of your life is up there," he began drawing in the air. "On the one side you've got 'was always on time' and on the other side there's 'allowed herself to be fully embraced by the moment.' Which would you choose?"

"I've read that stuff about being in the present moment. It sounds nice, but I just can't manage it for more than ten seconds before I start thinking about something I have to do."

He veered toward the water's edge, where the waves lapped in gentle white foam. He took her arm and moved her, so she would be on the outside edge of the water, and he would be protectively on the inside of the incoming waves. "Never take your eyes off the ocean. Even if it seems calm. You want to show the water you respect her."

"You think I might be in danger in one-inch waves?"

"It's just a gentlemanly habit."

"Well, it's a nice habit. I feel very safe."

April kicked up the water, to splash her calves. The water was cool, but after walking in the warm sun, it felt just right.

He smiled."Yeah. Now you're getting it."

"So, Now Time is just like being a little kid," she said.

"Kinda. It's like having a *fuller* moment."

"If there is a *now* time—is there a *then* time?" she teased.

"Um. I like that. Now and—*then there's Hawaii Time.*" He playfully splashed her ankles. She splashed him right back.

He stopped walking and seemed to be staring at a spot on the sand. She looked where he was looking, but she didn't see anything. He tilted his head and pointed. But she saw nothing.

"What? What do you see?" she asked.

"I see a perfect spot."

"For what?"

"For imagination."

He walked to a very specific spot on the sand. She liked having this moment to watch his strong back as he walked away. When she came up to join him he had already smoothed out an area of fresh clean sand with his hands. She watched for awhile trying to figure out what he was doing. A sand castle. He was making a sand castle.

"Hawaii Time may be perfect for building a sand castle on a perfect sunny day, but *New York Time* is no fun when you get stuck in the subway at rush hour, when the lights go out, and you have smelly strangers smashed up against you," she said. "It's hardly a moment I want to savor."

"And yet, if it is a situation you can't do anything about, you might as well submit to it. Enjoy a quiet, darkened moment." He looked up at her, "Are you going to help?"

"I don't exactly have expertise in castle building."

"You don't need a PhD to build a sand castle. Have a seat."

April knelt down on the sand next to him. She watched his actions and imitated what he was doing, pushing a wall of sand in his direction.

"First we make a foundation."

They worked together in silence. Occasionally her fingers brushed against his, which sent tiny currents up her arms. It made her work faster.

He stopped and watched her furiously moving large

amounts of sand. "Are we in a hurry?" he said with a wry smile.

"Sorry." She slowed down. Feeling a little silly, she tried to explain. "Quiet makes my mind race. I start thinking about my To Do List."

"It's a habit to have split-focus," he patiently explained. "But it robs you of being fully committed to any moment."

"'The Joys of Multi-Tasking. A Modern Epidemic,'" she said. "I read that article on the airplane."

"Yes, it's one thing to come to Hawaii," he said. "It's another thing *to arrive*."

"So how exactly am I supposed to magically be on Hawaii Time?"

"I'll show you. Hold your hands like this." He cupped his hands together, palms up, to demonstrate what he wanted her to do.

She put her hands up, matching his. He took a small amount of sand, and drizzled it very slowly, just a few grains at a time over her palms.

"Put all your attention on the sensation of a few grains of sand falling into your hands."

April brought all her awareness to the sensation he was creating. It did feel good, tingly and alive.

"I feel like my hands are waking up."

"I call that filling the senses. Then there's no room for all those jumbled thoughts."

April let that in. As best she could.

Some Japanese tourists about twenty yards down the beach had left their blanket too close to the water's edge. Kaikoa saw a bigger wave coming, and he leapt up and darted over to help just as the water began sucking their basket and all their belongings into the ocean.

April watched as he recovered their shoes, water bottles, magazines, and several plastic bags from the grips of the ocean. They all bowed and thanked him profusely. The older Japanese man offered money, but Kaikoa shook his head "no" and backed away. After much bowing, between the tourists and him, Kaikoa returned.

"That was very gallant of you."

"I did it for the turtles. Don't need all that junk in the water. Especially the plastic bags."

"You're the ocean's hero." April looked at him with a new kind of appreciation, but he just shrugged off the compliment.

"Okay, I've been thinking." April said, breaking the silence."

"I think you're always thinking."

"Unfortunately, that's true. I want to understand. Just explain it to me as simply as you can. What's the difference between your time and my time?"

"There are two main ways of relating to time. Now-time people relate to time as if the present moment is all there is," he paused and took a slow, gentle breath. "Linear-time people see time moving in one direction, like on a timeline."

"But that's how it is. Isn't that how everyone sees it?"

"Not everyone. Point to where the past is."

April didn't hesitate. She pointed behind her.

"Linear time people see the past as behind them. Like on a time line where they are marching away from the past toward the future."

"Where else would it be?" she said. "How else will you know if you are moving *toward* the future?"

Kaikoa nodded and used his finger in the sand to make a circle, widening the moat around the castle. "Having a vision for the future is okay but it's good to remember that the past is still alive, all around us, interacting with us. Our ancestors have a presence. The past has grace and it informs the present. It's more like a circle. It can widen to include more awareness. But the past isn't gone."

April studied him. She wondered what it was like to see time as a widening or contracting circle.

"Do you think our castle needs a turret?" he asked, breaking the silence.

April nodded, still trying to digest the idea of time as an ever-widening circle.

"How many turrets do we need?"

"One?"

"One. For a unified vision. That's deep," he said.

It sounded as if he thought she had said something truly profound, so she didn't want to tell him it was simply the first number that came to her mind.

He got up and scoured the area for items that might help him build the turret.

April shook her head, thinking to herself. *Strange the things that please him. He really did seem to have a certain peace of mind and playfulness that she had long lost.* She watched him gathering items on the beach. A piece of tree bark and a child's abandoned and broken red plastic pail which he filled with ocean water. Occasionally he would look up at her, happily displaying a prize item he had found, and she would nod in approval. He continued carefully searching, gathering up bits and pieces of colored glass and broken shells.

Kaikoa returned with his treasures, like a proud hunter

36

coming home to feed his pack. He used the water to make wet sand which he molded into the single turret in the center of the castle. He widened the moat, and went back several times to fill the pail and empty the water into the moat, until it looked like the real thing. Then they worked together to make a walkway lined with bits of shell. It was starting to look impressive.

April was getting more comfortable with these periods of silence. It meant she could watch him. She wondered if he could feel her gaze. Did he like being watched as much as she liked watching him?

The Japanese tourists approached, gesturing that they would like to take a picture of the castle he was building. Kaikoa nodded and leaned out of the frame. She wondered if he was like a Native American artist she had worked with who believed that having a photo taken meant someone took a piece of your soul. She made a mental note to look into this, as it would be important for Consolidated Branding's website, where they featured photos and artist bios. If he wasn't willing to have his photo on their website, she would have to make sure to include that as a line item in the contract.

The tourists took several photos of the castle and each other, and after more deep bows, left chattering away in the bubbly, fluid sounds of Japanese.

As soon as they were alone again, April's mind kicked back in.

"But the past *is* behind us," April said, as if they had just stopped talking a second ago. "It's over. Like when people we love die. We can't change it."

"I see it differently," he said. "To me it's not over and gone. The past is alive because I'm still constantly changing my relationship to it and with those who have passed."

April fell silent. Thinking about connecting with those who have passed left her brooding. She wasn't sure if she was ready to believe this possibility.

"Put your finger here," he said.

April placed her finger to help support the turret as he used the broken stone to create a textured pattern in the turret wall. It was intricate work, and made it more beautiful.

"When you say 'alive' – you don't mean as in *living now*?"

"Yes, I do."

"As in the zombie dead are walking amongst us?"

April smiled to make light of her effort at being funny, but Kaikoa took it entirely seriously. He stared over her shoulder in such a focused way that it sent a shiver up her spine.

"Don't turn around," he whispered.

April tried not to look but couldn't resist. She was about to turn around, when Kaikoa put up his hand to stop her.

"Don't look."

"Why not?"

"Just a minute more."

"Who's there?"

"Just . . . someone. Okay, you can look now."

April turned. There was no one there. There was no one for yards away. She turned back to Kaikoa. "Who was there?" She looked at the sand behind them. There were no footsteps.

Kaikoa went back to working a stick with his hands, carving a door in the castle.

The tiny hairs on April's arm were standing straight up and her skin had erupted in tiny bumps.

"In Hawaii we call that 'chicken skin.' It's when someone passes through from the other side. Makes the skin all jumpy."

"Are you going to explain it to me?"

"Yes. If you are going to be around me, you might as well understand…"

April wondered what he meant when he said *'If you're going to be around me.' Did he mean casually, in business, for the next couple of days, or for longer?* It all made her head feel that it was spinning slightly. Maybe it was the sun, or the sleeplessness.

"For me, my present includes a living past, he said. "Not just an imaginary one."

The sand on the front door of the castle wasn't wet enough, and the door he was making collapsed.

"You're thirsty."

April wasn't sure if he was talking to her, or the castle, as he poured more water on the door. She realized she was thirsty. She felt too dazed to move.

A pretty young mother and her two small children stopped to admire the castle. Kaikoa smiled and nodded back. "Uncle, who's it for?" the boy asked.

"A very special queen," Kaikoa said.

The kids looked back and forth between the castle and April.

"I allow visitors," April offered.

That seemed to satisfy them. They nodded and the mom waved them on.

"Do you think she's really a queen?" April heard the younger boy say, as they took off to catch up with their mom.

"Family?" April asked. He hadn't bothered with any

introductions.

"No. I forgot their names. I think we shared some waves. Once kids respect you in the water, they call you uncle."

"But focusing on the future is important. I read a study, from Harvard or someplace, where it said that people who have goals are more likely to achieve them."

"Uh, huh. I saw that on one of your company's coffee mugs that your boss sent me. But I don't believe the future is pre-set. It's not solid like a mountain, and anyway a mountain only appears to be solid. It's always changing, just at a slower rate." He stopped working and sat back to observe his work.

"It's beautiful."

"And temporary."

Kaikoa suddenly reached out his arm and leveled the castle.

"Hey," April yelled. "You just spent all this time building—"

"I didn't *spend* it. I borrowed it."

"A queen needs her castle," April said with a mock pout.

"I'll build you another one."

"I liked *that* one."

"Life is change. You can't get too attached to form."

"Especially to a sand castle."

Kaikoa worked his hands quickly, like a potter with wet clay, to smooth the sand over the entire area.

"I can't believe you just erased it. Now there's no trace of our castle."

Kaikoa surveyed the flat area. He rolled his arm over the sand to create small peaks and valleys and variations in the surface. "I like that more," he said as he studied the sand. "This is just as beautiful. The empty space is full of possibility."

He adjusted it further with his fingers, creating subtle ridges.

April laughed. "Artists!"

"Yeah, we always see the world through different lenses. Let's go get you a cool drink."

As they walked back toward the Paradise Resort Café, she noticed that his eyes were always drawn to the distant waves. "Do you like to paint the ocean?"

This made him laugh. "I'm not that crazy."

"What's crazy about that? The waves are beautiful, and colorful. Lot's of artists paint the ocean."

"I'm not 'lots of artists.'"

"I wasn't trying to offend you."

"I'm not offended."

"What are you?"

"Misunderstood."

He stopped for a moment, his toes rolling over a tiny smooth dark rock lodged in the wet sand. The water lapped at his feet as his big toe seemed to be "reading" the rock. April stood very still next to him, a little further back, not wanting to interrupt his internal process. She studied him carefully, trying to read his body language. She needed a little better insight so she wouldn't step on his strange, mercurial artist's sensibilities. She was definitely going to have to bring her "A" game to this negotiation. She sensed he was a patient teacher, and maybe a good strategy would be for her to be a willing student. "So why do you study the waves, but won't paint them?"

"You can't capture a moment on canvas. You can watch the overall motion. But if you try to capture a specific wave, it's a lie. A true wave is always changing, swirling, merging. It's like trying to paint the future. A future that is as fluid as these waves in front of us."

"Each individual wave is changing," she said with authority. "But I can look at the ocean and see a constant body of water."

Kaikoa laughed. "I can't imagine seeing it as a constant. Now you're going to tell me you don't believe in global warming."

"I'm as worried about global warming as the next person. But what about getting ahead? You can't just muddle through life without a plan."

"Getting ahead is okay. But not if it is in the way of *getting a life.*"

His attention went to a surfer riding a long wave. Kaikoa leaned to the right, slightly, as if he were riding the wave with the surfer, then to the left a fraction of a moment before the surfer did.

"Why did you destroy the sand castle?"

"To remind us that everything changes."

* * *

They walked up to the edge of the café. Guests lay on lounges by the pool, their exposed skin oiled up, asleep in the warm sun. Kaikoa stopped at the edge of the low fence. April stared at the guests. It felt like the two of them didn't belong in this sedentary scene.

A waiter in a tropical shirt waved to them and pointed to an empty table.

"How thirsty are you?" Kaikoa asked.

"Well," she sensed he didn't want to park there. "Not very."

"You're not a very good liar."

A young waiter, passing by with a tray of full water glasses with a slice of lemon on the side, exchanged a nod with Kaikoa. He came over. Kaikoa took two tall glasses of cool water and handed both to April. "We'll be back. Save us that table in front when they leave."

The waiter gave Kaikoa a nod and the "shaka" hand signal. April had read about that gesture on the airplane magazine. It literally means "hang loose" but locals use it to mean "*it's cool,* or *no problem,* or *we're local,*" or almost any friendly message desired and somehow known by the person on the receiving end.

April had already downed one glass of water when she thought to offer Kaikoa the second one.

"You need it more than I do," he said. "Drink up."

April was surprised that she could swallow the whole second glass. "Wow. Guess I was thirsty."

Kaikoa smiled.

It seemed that he had a better idea of what she needed than she did.

"Come on, there's something we have to do before we lie down like lizards." He gestured and she followed him back toward the waves.

"I don't suppose you're going to tell me."

"I would tell you. But I don't know. It hasn't happened yet."

"I wish I could live like that. I mean, I wish I was the kind of girl who could just whip off her pareo and jump into the waves. I wish I didn't care what strangers on a beach think

43

of me. I wish I could tell my boss to take a hike. I wish a lot of things. But my reality is filled with future appointments. Rent that's due on the first day of the month. And credit card bills with penalties for not paying them on due dates. And how can you be happy without planning, and having future goals?" She looked over at Kaikoa, half hoping he would talk her out of everything she had just said. But he just looked at her, the way an artist studies a face.

"So if you're not the tear-off-the-pareo kind of girl maybe you're the peel-off kind." He tugged on the edge of the fabric ever so slightly, but enough to loosen the knot that held her cover together.

"Stop," she said with little conviction in her voice. All this intense conversation had left her feeling really warm, and the water did look inviting.

"Even if I stopped now, it's already loose."

It was true. The knot slid open and she tugged the fabric away from his strong hand.

"Please?" His voice had a sweet pleading tone she wouldn't have imagined. "We have to take your new bikini for a test drive." He looked her over. "So far it's taking the curves just fine. But we really don't know until it gets wet."

"Wait." She put on the breaks.

"For what?"

"I don't know." She searched for an excuse and suddenly remembered her real purpose. "Maybe we should take a look at the contract first."

"I don't think water and contracts mix."

He took a corner of the pareo and tied it around his wrist. Then he backed away from her slowly, gently pulling her toward the waves.

The dance was on. What else could she do but follow his lead?

Ulu-Breadfruit

Chapter Three

When she finally emerged from the water, her body felt cleansed from the warm ocean. Every step was slow and delicious in the sinking sand. She sighed deeply, leaving behind a year of stress.

She looked back. He was emerging right behind her, shaking his long, wavy, wet hair. She knew he would be right there as he had been swimming and floating near her the whole time she was in the water. She could feel his eyes on her as she walked, and she liked the feeling of him watching her hips move.

"What?" She asked of his mischievous smile.

"You surprised me."

"How?"

"You were like a mermaid in the water."

"What were you expecting?"

"I thought you would be a one-toe-in-at-a-time kind of girl. But you just dove in, and bobbed and rode the waves like you were born in the water."

"I spent summers at my uncle's house on Long Island. Those were happy days."

"When was the last time you were in the ocean?"

"He died when I was sixteen. His daughter sold the house. Guess it's been awhile."

"We'll have to make up for lost time," he said, and she saw a look of sadness she hadn't seen before.

"I didn't think "now time" people could lose time," she said.

"Good point." He smiled and led her to the outdoor shower faucets on the ledge above the sand.

"You were hovering like a lifeguard. Did you think I couldn't swim?"

"I wanted to see how the water reacted to you."

He turned on her shower faucet. It was cold but invigorating as she washed the salt and sand away. There is nothing like an outdoor shower to make you feel natural and free. He rinsed off next to her. His movements were efficient, like one who is conscious of not wasting water. She couldn't help sneaking peeks at his strong back. His body was perfectly toned like the surfer he was. She knew from his bio that he was thirty-nine years old, but he still had the muscle tone he had in his surfing competition pictures. She had seen a picture on the internet of him holding a Koa wood bowl trophy when he was twenty-two, surfing on an ocean preservation charity team.

"I'm going to get us some chairs," he said. He turned off his water faucet, hard. She liked that he was conscious about not wasting water. She quickly finished rinsing out her long hair, and turned off her faucet. When she swung around, he was standing there, holding the hotel's fluffy beach towel for her.

"Perfect timing." She shivered with the chill of being wet.

"We're over there." He pointed to two chaise lounges under a pink flowered umbrella by the hotel pool. The chaises were pointed to face the perfect view of the ocean.

She noticed her pareo was draped on the chair. "Thanks. I had forgotten all about it."

"I could open a store with all the things that get forgotten on the beach," he said.

"That was nice of you to go get it."

As usual, he just shrugged off the compliment. He led her over to their spot, and she settled into the chaise with that wonderfully good tired feeling of having worked out the lungs and the heart and swimming muscles that she hadn't used in years.

A poolside waiter appeared. "What can I get you to drink?" he asked.

April looked at Kaikoa to see if he was going to have anything.

"It's your first day in Hawaii, it is mandatory to have a tall drink with a paper umbrella. In case there's a paper rain, you don't want to be caught without your paper umbrella."

The waiter laughed.

She liked that Kaikoa was the kind of person who would take a moment to entertain a waiter. The men in New York that she dined with thought themselves above chatting, much less entertaining the waiters.

"And you're not allowed to leave our hotel without having imbibed at least three of our famous Mai Tai's," the waiter said to April.

"Well, then I better get started. I wouldn't want to fall

behind."

"Two Mai-Tai's, please."

"Light or heavy?" the waiter asked.

"I'll go with heavy," she said.

"Better go with light. You haven't slept much."

"I can handle the full experience."

"Be careful what you ask for. You will get it."

April read far too much into that comment to reply.

"You better eat some protein with that." He turned to the waiter. "Two Mahi-Mahi sandwiches. And two heavy Mai-Tai's."

The waiter seemed relieved to now have a clear order. April wouldn't admit it to him, but she liked that Kaikoa ordered for her. She never knew what to order in new places and usually ordered the wrong thing.

Kaikoa leaned back and closed his eyes. He wasn't the kind of guy who had to fill every moment of silence with excess words. She closed her eyes too, and must have drifted off into an easy dreamy ride, because when she woke up, the waiter was placing the drinks on the little table between the lounges.

She took her first sip. The rum drink, flavored with orange and almond, was strong but gentle on the throat. The sweet, juicy tropical flavors made everything seem right with the world. "Oh, My God, that is amazing."

"Are you two on your honeymoon?" the waiter asked, with a broad hospitality smile.

April choked. Her mind went into guilty high gear. Apparently she didn't look like a tough New York businesswoman on a mission to get a deal signed.

"Not yet," Kaikoa offered the waiter, with a big "it's

okay" shaka hand sign.

The waiter gave a relieved bob of his head. Clearly the shaka reassured him that he hadn't done something terribly wrong.

"Oh, sorry. I didn't . . ." The waiter fumbled for the right words. "You two just looked so happy. Well, let me know if you need anything else."

Kaikoa bit into his fish sandwich, unfazed by this moment. April was still trying to get her mind to remember where square one was. "Maybe I should go to my room and bring down a copy of the contract." She got to her feet but he motioned for her to stay.

"Eat. While it's still warm."

She sat back down. She was hungry. As they ate she used the quiet between them to gather her thoughts. The warm, tender mahi-mahi fish was good, and the sweet and tangy rum drink was even better. She could feel it going to her brain, softening the edges. The turquoise pool in front of them with a fountain was like a tranquility pill. The mosaic of a turtle on the bottom shimmered with the soft breeze.

He didn't chatter through the meal. Most of her meals in New York were lunch or dinner meetings, and you never got to really taste or digest the food while trying to navigate through business negotiations. It was a relief to just eat and enjoy the flavors.

The tangy sauce on the fish sandwich was so savory it hit the palette in all the right places.

"Those are local Waimanalo greens, it's *ono.*" Kaikoa said, as April enjoyed the colorful fresh salad. "*Ono* means tastes really good," he explained.

It wasn't long before her plate was clean. When they

were both finished eating, to her surprise, he brought up business.

"How many pages is this contract?"

"Twenty-eight. I can go get it—"

"Twenty-eight! That will take me a week to read."

"It's really just our standard boiler plate, with a few specific additions for Asia."

"Did you read it?" he asked.

"Of course."

"Then summarize it for me."

He pulled his sunglasses over his eyes and settled back on the chaise as if this was going to be a bedtime story.

"I can't summarize twenty-eight pages. You need to read it for yourself."

"I'm not going to read it, unless I know I'm interested in signing it. So you can either summarize it or go home with an unsigned contract." His tone wasn't rude, but it left no room for ambiguity.

"Should I take it that you're not interested in making money from your art?" She was used to artists putting up a strong front before getting down to business. Some of them had to create an elaborate "I don't do this for the money" ruse. Yet, they were almost always struggling financially, and one deal with Consolidated Branding would change their lifestyle. She saw herself as someone who could make dreams come true for those who were willing to play along with the commercial game. But she knew that not all artists were willing to play in that arena. She felt fairly certain which type Kaikoa was.

"Not if it means turning my art into smiley faces on Wal-Mart bags."

April sat straight up and turned to face him, her brain

suddenly clicking into gear. This was going to be a serious business conversation after all. "Our company, Consolidated Branding, licenses the work of artists for various corporate clients. They use these images for internal marketing. Everything from calendars, coffee mugs, key chains, promotional items. Because of the deals we've negotiated, some of our artists have become their own International brands. Several of our artists make up to two-hundred and fifty thousand a year in royalty fees—"

"So you own me," he interrupted, "And I end up on SWAG."

"We buy specific images that we sell and re-use. Of course you own everything else you create, but naturally we ask you not to license very similar images."

"Basically, you want to turn me into a coffee-mug artist."

"You are free to do all the rest of your art in any way you please. We don't interfere with your creative process. The contract will specify which exact images we are licensing."

"Is this a forever license? Not that it matters, since you can't re-sell stuff once it has been branded as coffee-mug SWAG."

"It is a five-year initial contract," she explained. "So we are taking quite a risk with you—that your images will hold their value. After that we have the option of first refusal, for another five years."

Kaikoa sat up, took off his sunglasses, and looked straight at her. "I explained to your boss, Colonel Morgan, that I was not for sale."

A cold feeling slithered up her spine. "We do not own you," she improvised quickly. "Many of our artists have told us that Consolidated Branding frees them up to paint what they like, because they have a source of income. They don't have to try to paint to please the market, or a gallery owner. Outside of the images you license to us, you are your own boss."

"Name me one of your artists."

"What? Well, they are not well-known."

"Exactly. They have compromised themselves into obscurity."

"Is being famous important to you?" April asked, "Because if that is your career trajectory, we can develop a strategy that—" His stone-cold expression made it clear this was not what he wanted.

"April, you are perceptive enough to tell that I am not interested in this deal."

She took a hard breath, stealing her nerves. "All contracts are negotiable," she said, swallowing hard. "If you tell me what your concerns are, perhaps we can come to some kind of understanding that works for both of us." She managed to keep her voice steady but a stream of cool sweat ran down her cheek, betraying her.

"April, I paint because I have a relationship with Nature. My paintings are a reflection of that relationship. If I sell out those images to become a Consolidated Brand, it is like being unfaithful to my true love. I'm not sure I could live with myself." He stood up. The meeting was over.

"Wait."

"For what?"

"At least have dinner with me tonight." She tried, hoping he couldn't hear her heart thumping in her throat.

"There's nothing that you can say that is going to convince me." He held out his hand to shake hers. "I believe we've come to an impasse. Goodbye, Miss Walton."

April didn't take his hand. She felt a panic she couldn't explain. "Okay, but maybe we could still have dinner. Together. I'm on an expense account. I'm supposed to take you out." April was dancing in quicksand and every moment was sucking her lower.

"Give me one good reason why we should have dinner together."

"Because I don't know anybody in Hawaii."

He studied her.

She wished she hadn't had the heavy drink. She willed herself not to cry. After the highs of their day together this moment felt like an all time low. She swore to herself not to let him any nearer to her heart. She was obviously not prepared for the ride.

After an incredibly brutal silence, he said, "On one condition."

"Name it."

"Absolutely no talk about business."

She nodded.

"Agreed?" he looked her straight in the eye.

"Agreed."

Kaikoa pulled on his T shirt.

"What time are we meeting?" she asked.

"At sunset."

"Where shall I meet you?"

"At the watch graveyard."

"The what?"

"Where we buried your obsession with time."

He turned and walked away. He didn't look back.

Chapter Four

"Aloha, Leilani."

April was glad to see a familiar face, even if that person was never going to get her name right.

Mildred waved her inside the store. "How did Kaikoa like the new bikini?"

"I don't know," April said, feeling a little shaky from the encounter with him moments ago, even more than from the Mai Tai. "He didn't mention anything about it."

Mildred smiled and wagged her finger at April. "You can't expect a man to tell you his feelings *with words*. Where were his eyes?"

"I guess they went to all the right places," April admitted.

"Ah, if you only listen with your *ears,* you won't hear with your heart." Mildred patted her own heart.

"Well, he did kind of drink me in." April just now realized this was true.

Mildred clapped her hands in satisfaction. "That's what I'm telling you."

"You were right."

Mildred went behind the counter and produced a shopping bag with April's clothes.

"That phone of yours. Ring, ring, ring. I had to turn it off." Mildred handed her the bag of clothes she had left earlier. They were folded nicely and wrapped in tissue paper as if they were a new purchase. April was embarrassed that her running clothes were given such nice treatment.

"Thanks. I hardly brought anything. If I showed up at work with anything more than my usual carry-on, my boss would worry that I was going on vacation."

"Did he invite you to dinner?"

April squelched the impulse to lie. "Actually, I invited him."

"Very modern." Mildred said, but April caught the wary look.

"Begged him was more like it."

"Sometimes men need a little nudge, eh?"

"Eh. Yes."

"What are you wearing?'

April answered with a blank look.

"No worries. I fix you."

"I need fixing," April muttered.

Mildred was already in motion, expertly moving through the racks of clothes.

Since her boss was supposed to have come to Hawaii to sign Kaikoa to Consolidated Branding, April had less than twelve hours notice for this trip. She had been all packed to meet another artist in Colorado, when she got the call at home at 5 AM that her boss couldn't make it, and she was to switch assignments. Kristy, her co-worker, headed for Colorado, and April on the red-eye to Hawaii that night. She hadn't time to re-pack, as she had an early morning meeting, so she had taken her usual carry-on with two business suits, three silk blouses, and her work out clothes. She had nothing for a dinner in Paradise.

"Here, this is perfect." Mildred said, holding up a lovely black dress with a pattern of red hibiscus flowers. It was that silky natural cotton and had a wonderful feminine flow, with twisted shoulder straps and a flattering V neckline. April loved it at first sight.

"Try it on." Mildred ordered delightedly. "Perfect for your Honu necklace." She pointed to the delicate turtle charm around her neck. "I'll find you some sandals."

"I'm a—"

"I remember. Seven and half. Feet don't grow from going in the ocean."

When April emerged from the dressing room, Mildred already had a pair of slip on mules with a strand of black and red jeweled beads—very demure and elegant.

"How much are these?"

Mildred smiled at her choice. "Don't worry, I give you Kama'aina discount."

"What is that?"

"Kama'aina. It's only for locals. You friend of Kaikoa, you might become one. Wear your hair up. That way he can think about how he will get it down." Mildred burst into a rippling giggle that made April laugh with her.

"Sounds like you know Kaikoa pretty well."

"It's a small island," Mildred said. "But I wouldn't

want to paint it."

* * *

April decided to treat herself to a pedicure. The first one in years. As she sat in the massage chair with the drying pads between her toes, she remembered she hadn't turned on her cell phone.

Five new messages from her boss. Of course. She didn't bother listening to them; she just dialed back.

"Did he sign?" Dana was not the kind of person who bothered with normal pleasantries such as hello and goodbye.

"You didn't tell me he turned you down."

"I didn't want to prejudice you going in. I know if anybody can turn this deal right side up it's you."

April smiled. Her boss sparingly used well calculated praise. And it usually worked. She set aside her frustration with Dana's leaving her in the dark that Kaikoa had already turned down the deal.

"How did he react to the contract?" Dana could switch back to business faster than a hummingbird.

"He hasn't read it yet, but—"

"Why hasn't he read it?"

"We just had our first meeting. I think this deal is going to need some massaging."

April heard Dana's exasperated exhale, and imagined her standing at her desk; she rarely sat. She was always in motion, doing a desk push up, or core exercise, which she did while on her headset phone, to burn excess calories, which she didn't need to lose. By the end of most days, she had gotten in a solid workout without leaving her desk.

"Tell me you're making progress. It's been four hours since we last spoke, and I can't have you incommunicado that long. Especially with the time zone difference. You've lost a whole day."

"He asked me to summarize the deal points."

"You summarized a twenty-eight page contract?" Dana didn't make much of a distinction between a question and a statement. "Then where are we? Are we anything near close?"

"I'm working on it." She cupped her hand around the phone in an attempt to hide the happy Hawaiian music playing in the background in the salon.

"Probably working on getting your nails done. I recognize that music in the salon."

April cursed to herself silently. Her boss called it *situational awareness*. She had more than anyone.

"You know I'll be reading your expense report."

"As always. You will know my every move."

"April, tell me you've got this deal on the rails—heading in the right direction."

"I'm working it," was all April could manage.

"I assume you're having dinner with him tonight. Take your cell phone. And leave it on."

"Okay." In spite of the relaxing music, April struggled to make her voice match her boss's intensity.

"And if you're going to buy a pretty dress, bring me back some Kona coffee." Dana was gone without any words of polite closure.

"Aloha to you, too," April said to the dial tone.

She was about to go back to her room when she noticed a boutique in the lobby with a sign reading: "French Lingerie Sale—Two for One—Today Only." *They probably have that sign up every day.* But April backtracked and went inside.

Moments later she emerged with two sets of black lace panties and a matching bra in a small pink shopping bag. *I can't believe I just bought lingerie.*

Was it bad luck to buy sexy new lingerie before a first date?

Wait. This is not a date. She was tempted to turn right around and return them. But the receipt read "No return on sale items." *Oh, well. It's been eons since I bought any nice lingerie.* Having new lingerie always made a new dress feel more exciting.

April stopped at the hotel's front desk. A smiling woman, with *Pua* written on her name tag, stepped up to help her.

"Excuse me," said April, "I'm supposed to meet someone, and he told me to meet him at Sunset. What time is that exactly?"

"Did he mean *before* sunset, *during* sunset or *after* sunset?"

April's spirits sank even lower. That was a distinction she hadn't even considered.

"Are you meeting a local person?" she asked.

April nodded.

A local Hawaiian bellboy, overhearing their conversation, chimed in. "When the sky starts to look like a painting," he said, and went off to carry some bags.

"I'd say around 6:30 would be a good idea," Pua offered.

April thanked her, and headed up to her room. She felt the tug of a nap calling to her. She just hoped she could turn off her mind long enough to let the nap win.

* * *

By six o'clock April felt like an exposed wire. She had been ready for half an hour. She couldn't decide whether to wear her hair up as Mildred had suggested, or down, and had gone back and forth twice. She wasn't good at these small decisions. Having her hair up did feature her turtle necklace, which he seemed to admire the first time he saw her, so she finally decided to go with that choice. She wished she had a pretty comb or flower for her hair, but she couldn't do anything about that now. Pacing around in her room was not doing anything good for her nerves, so she headed downstairs to the beach and looked around.

He wasn't there. She wasn't sure she knew exactly where *their spot* was. She looked for evidence of the wrist watch graveyard, but she wasn't sure she was even looking in the right place. Or even exactly what time *sunset* really is. It would be so much easier if he had just given her a specific time. *Linear time certainly has plenty of advantages when it comes to making plans with other people.* She was already more than a little frustrated with his vague time references and concepts like *Hawaii Time*.

She slipped out of her shoes and surveyed the sand, looking everywhere for the shell that Kaikoa had placed to mark the spot where he buried her watch. The shell must have gotten tipped over, or crushed, and buried with all the vacationers coming and going, oblivious to the watch-gravesite they were defacing.

Not wanting to sit on the sand in her new dress, she knelt down where she thought it might be, and smoothed over the area with the palms of her hands. She was just about to give up hope of finding it when her big toe felt something. She scooped away a bit of sand, and there it was; the small white, slightly chipped shell with the purple edge that he had used to mark the spot.

So pleased to find it, she held it next to her heart and closed her eyes. This shell felt more valuable than a brick of gold. Something about the odds of finding one shell on a whole wide beach made everything in the universe seem suddenly orderly.

Then she felt a shadow near her. She opened her eyes, and he was standing there, watching her. She blushed, and wondered how long he had been there. Was it long enough to see her hugging a broken shell to her heart?

He wore a black Aloha shirt embroidered with a red dragon. It was both elegant and casual. His hair seemed neater than usual.

"I like how you used your hands when your eyes couldn't find the shell," he said.

"What are the chances of finding a single small white shell on a white sandy beach?"

"If you know how to look, the chances are quite good."

He sat down next to her, and turned to face the ball of fire that was slowly sinking in the sky. The ever changing canvas of colors before them was hypnotic, but his presence was even more compelling. What was a magnificent sunset compared to the sensations he evoked in her?

"It's called *po'ailani.*" He said pointing to the horizon line they were both gazing at. "Watching it slide away is the Hawaiian antidote to stress."

"I can see why," April said. Its magic was working its

way into every cell of her body.

Without turning to her, he said, "You look like a dream in that dress."

She was glad his eyes were on the sky, because her cheeks were as crimson as the sun.

"This is for you. It's from my backyard." He pulled a red hibiscus flower from the pocket of his Aloha shirt.

Had it been next to his heart? He handed her the flower. The petals were delicate and warm. Even though it had gotten slightly crushed in his pocket, it was the most perfect flower she had ever seen.

"Put it in your hair," he suggested.

She wasn't ready to put it someplace where she couldn't see it, but she tried to stick it in her bun.

"Put it on the right side."

"Why?"

"The left side means you're married."

"I never said if I was married or not."

"Male instinct," he said. "If you are available, you wear it on your right."

She placed the flower over her right ear.

He smiled. "I'm going to have to watch over you like a hawk. Can't have every beach boy in Waikiki trailing after you."

April laughed.

He looked around, as if he was on guard.

"I think you can relax the heat seeking missiles. I haven't been on a date in over a year," April said, without thinking of the consequences of such an admission.

Ironically, at that moment a young, tanned lifeguard walked by, and turned to look at April with the flower over her right ear. Then he looked at Kaikoa, who stared him down, and the lifeguard kept walking. She had forgotten about that kind of territorial protective energy from a man.

Kaikoa turned back to her, with his intense eyes.

"Maybe this is better." He reached over and took the flower from her right side and placed it over her left ear. That seemed to relax him.

The touch of his arm brushing against her cheek sent tingles everywhere. *Did he feel them too?*

"Let's walk." He stood and held out a gallant hand to help her up. "We'll find the best spot to watch the day slide into a perfect night. It happens really quickly," he said. "If you blink, you could miss the green flash." He pointed to the horizon line just as the sun was hitting the water line.

"Why do they call it the green flash?" she asked.

"Keep looking."

"You're making this up. Is this just a joke you play on tourists?

"No. The Green Flash is real. It's a fleeting burst of intense emerald light. The secret is to look away for a quick second so the sun won't imprint its image on your retina. When only the very top of the sun's disk is about to disappear below the horizon—then you look back. Go ahead, turn away."

April turned away from the sun. He continued to watch for the top of the sun's crown to slide further down into the ocean.

"How will I know when to turn back?"

"I'll tell you. And when I say 'look' turn back quickly."

April was impatient. She stared at him to keep her mind occupied.

"Now?"

"I'll tell you when."

The light was dimming by the second, and her mischievous side wanted to cheat and look at the sun now.

"But you're staring into the sun; won't that ruin it for you?"

"I've seen it several times. This one is for you."

"Are you sure you're not making this up?"

He pointed to other people, both tourists and locals, who had lined up along the ocean edge, watching and waiting.

"The same physics that makes the rainbow makes the green flash," he explained.

"I always wanted to know how rainbows happen."

"It happens when rays of sunlight enter a raindrop."

"Is that why you usually see them just after a light rain?" she asked.

"Yes. The light from the sun is made up of a spectrum of colors, and they bounce around inside the raindrops and then exit."

"That's neat to think about light exiting."

"Each ray exits or is bent by different degrees. It's called dispersion. This unequal bending of sunlight is what sends out the rainbow of colors."

"You sound like a science teacher. How do you know so much?"

"When I was a teenager, I was the volunteer science tutor for eleven younger cousins. They would look up stuff just to try to trick me. I had to know my stuff or they would pulverize me."

"That's why you're so good with kids."

As usual he ignored the compliment.

"What does that have to do with the Green Flash?" she

asked.

"Light-bending is also what makes the Green Flash happen. Because the color green is bent most at sunset."

"Can I look now? I don't want to miss it."

"Don't you trust me to tell you when to look?"

"Yes. But I'm a New Yorker. Impatience is in our blood."

"With that kind of blood, I wouldn't want to be a vampire in New York."

She laughed and almost peeked but he held up a hand to prevent her.

"I can see I am going to have to be very patient with your impatience."

"How much longer?"

"About twenty seconds. You think you can last that long?"

"I just want to be ready."

"My little impatient mermaid. You know what Jules Verne said about the Green Flash in 1882?"

"Something like, 'Don't look too late'?"

"He called it 'Le Rayon Vert' which he said was 'a green which no artist could ever obtain on his palette. It is the color of Hope.'"

"Wow. I didn't realize—"

"Now," he said and grasped her hand. "Look."

She turned.

"Did you see it?"

"Uhhhmmm." She stared into the space where the sun had been but she was blinded by something else. The sensation of his warm hand on hers obliterated all her other senses.

Chapter Five

The upstairs dining patio of the Paradise Resort overlooked the ocean. It was lined with fiery torches and tall, bright Red Ginger plants. The gentle harmonies of loosened guitar strings of Hawaiian slack key music wafted up from the garden below.

April's taste buds were ignited by the Asian style opakapaka, a delicate steamed fish with shredded spring onion, ginger and cilantro, finished with sizzling peanut oil and drizzled with a splash of *shoyu* sauce and toasted sesame oil glaze.

"This is the perfect choice. I think I should let you order all my meals for the rest of my life," April said. She coughed nervously realizing the gravity of her words, and was relieved he didn't react to them.

"Try a taste of my Butterfish Misoyaki."

He fed her a piece off his fork, which was a trusting and intimate move. She wasn't normally someone who shared food like this, but he made it seem so natural.

"Umm. It's so tender. What kind of sauce is that?"

"Miso. It's a local favorite."

"Oh, my God, it's delicious."

"You just broil it briefly, that's how you get this browned and bubbling topping."

"You really seem to know about food. Are you a chef?"

"I can find my way around the kitchen."

"I don't even have one, April admitted. "Just two burners and a mini refrigerator."

Kaikoa stared at her.

Was he feeling sorry for her? If so, he didn't say it.

"It's fine. I manage," she said. "I'm not home for many meals. At work we have breakfast meetings, lunch meetings, and often have dinner brought in. Consolidated Branding feeds us so much as a way of making up for the fact that they control our lives." She was babbling again, but his concerned look had tripped something in her heart, and she pedaled fast. "I never know what to order in restaurants. I usually let my guest order first, and then say 'I'll have what he's having.'" April thought she saw a flicker of reaction to the word *he*, so she added, "Or *she's* having. These are business meetings." *Did I imagine this reaction? No, I saw something. I think.*

He said nothing for awhile, and finished the last of his fish.

"All those business meetings," he said. "I would think you would be an expert at ordering off strange menus."

"Too many choices in Manhattan. I just end up ordering the same things because I'm too lazy to try something

69

new."

"Somehow lazy is not a word I would use to describe you."

"Are you 100% Hawaiian?"

"Half-Hawaiian. Half Lolo."

When she didn't get it, he explained, "*Lolo* means crazy."

The waiter came and cleared their empty plates. Kaikoa gave the waiter a nod.

"I took the liberty of ordering you my favorite dessert," he said.

April beamed. He could make things so easy. *When he wanted to.*

"I'll be right back with the dessert," the waiter said and grinned at Kaikoa.

"Do you know every waiter in this town?"

"I grew up here. I've surfed with most of them. We've shared some gnarly waves."

"So, you were born and raised on the island of O'ahu and lived here your whole life?"

"Would you believe in the same house? Although house is not the word my school mates would use to describe it. As kids, we got teased a lot because of where we live. "

"What do you mean?" April said, imagining the worst.

"It's kind of historical. Ancestral is the nice way of putting it. They called it the 'Bone Yard.' It's a small old Chinese cemetery. My family has been the caretakers for three generations. Does that freak you out?"

"No, as long as the residents don't walk around at night."

"Only on certain full moons."

"I was kidding." But now April wasn't sure if *he* had been.

"It's quite beautiful. Especially during the full moons."

"It would be nice to see it sometime."

He looked at her and she wondered if her comment was too forward. Just as she contemplated a linguistic retreat, the waiter brought them the decadent, dark molten chocolate dessert and two spoons. The round warm cake was topped with vanilla ice-cream and two plump raspberries with a sprig of bright green mint.

They studied the culinary work laid before them. She stared at the perfectly formed, multi-faceted fruit. Ever since she was a little girl she had loved raspberries because they made everything seem sweet in the world. She used to put them on the top of two fingertips and have conversations between them. Remembering this game made her smile.

"Is there any color in the universe more perfect than the color of a raspberry?" he said, as if he had a key to the private vault in her mind.

Their eyes met. She wanted to say that he had nearly read her thoughts, but she was afraid it would compromise the magic. A slow smile played on his face.

"What?" she asked in answer to his gaze, "What are you thinking?"

"I was just wondering if you were the kind of girl who eats the raspberry first or saves it for last."

"I save it for last," she said. "What kind of boy are you?"

"Life is short. I'm an 'eat the raspberry first' kind of boy."

"I see. That way if there is a sudden Tsunami, at least

you will have had your raspberry."

"Exactly. Tell you what. Let's switch roles. I'll eat my raspberry last and you eat your raspberry first." He had that twinkle in his eye. There was clearly more to this game than he was saying.

"Have you carefully considered the consequences of altering the patterns of our personalities in such a drastic way?" she teased.

"Deeply."

The waiter noticed they hadn't touched the dessert, and the vanilla ice-cream was melting over the cake. "Is everything okay?" he asked.

"Everything is perfect," Kaikoa said to the waiter without taking his eyes off April.

The waiter faded away.

April picked up the raspberry on her side of the plate. She raised it to her lips. But she couldn't bring herself to devour it, with him watching her so carefully. She laughed at her own sudden shyness.

"How about if we both eat simultaneously," she said.

"That wasn't the rules."

"What rules? You just made them up."

"Well, you can make up the rules for the next game," he teased.

She took a deep breath and put the soft fruit inside her mouth. A burst of flavor hit her taste buds. Delicious soft wetness. He watched as her eyes closed to enjoy it even more fully. When she opened her eyes, she saw he had been watching her, mesmerized by her pleasure.

"You did that so nicely," he said quietly. "You ate that raspberry in Hawaii Time."

Then, as if to dissipate the building energy between them, they turned to the cake in front of them. April took the first bite, and he followed. They shared the cake, eating together in silence, but watching each other carefully. April didn't realize she began eating the cake faster, in anticipation of being able to watch him eat *his* raspberry.

Finally, he took the raspberry and balanced it on the tip of his finger.

"I can't believe you just did that."

"What?"

"Put the raspberry on your finger. I used to do that when I was a kid. I used to do it with two fingers—and have little conversations. Don't tell me you used to do that too."

"I've never done it before now." His eyes fixated on her necklace.

"Are you going to eat that raspberry?" she said boldly, "Otherwise you should worry that I might just snatch it away and gobble it up."

"You really think you could get it away from me?"

"I can. And I will. If you don't eat it. Quickly."

"I can. And I will. And I do intend to eat it. Sloooowly."

He moved the bright red raspberry closer to his lips in extreme slow motion. He licked his lips in anticipation. April felt herself blush. His lips pouted, he inhaled, slowly sucking the raspberry inside his lips, but held it softly between them a long moment.

* * *

After dinner, he led her downstairs towards the water. She enjoyed the silence between them. It gave her time to replay the memory of the raspberry on his lips. She had never met a man who was so good at savoring the tiny moments that most men race through.

He was looking up, studying the moon, which was a large ball of light in the sky.

"Is it a full moon tonight?" April asked.

"Almost. Tomorrow it will be."

They walked along the edge of the water. Kaikoa had taken their shoes and hidden them under a favorite bush. April wondered if it was safe to leave her purse next to them. It would be nice to have nothing to carry.

"Is it safe to leave my purse with the shoes? I could never leave a purse unattended—or even a pair of shoes in New York."

Kaikoa looked around. There were just a handful of others out for a stroll. He inhaled the air and shook his head *no*.

"Tonight has just a hint of danger" he said. "Better take it along."

April tucked her purse back under her arm.

"You can smell danger?"

"Sometimes. Sometimes it's just pork chops cooking."

She laughed. "Do you ever wear a watch?"

"No."

"There must be sometimes when you need to know what time it is."

"I just look up at the sun, and can usually tell what time it is, give or take."

"What happens when it rains?"

"Oh, well, when it rains, who cares what time it is?"

She laughed.

"Your world is so different from mine. I probably look

at my watch twenty times a day. I'm always juggling appointments, and calculating the travel time between them, or when I have to leave to arrive on time."

"I live in Hawaii Time. That means I get there when I get there."

"I've noticed."

"Try it sometime. You'll discover what's really important."

"Doesn't it drive other people crazy? I mean if they are waiting for you?"

"Only if they're on Ha'ole Time."

"That's the derogatory term for white people like me, right?"

"Ha'ole means people who don't breathe deeply."

"You wouldn't want to breathe so deeply if you lived in the center of Manhattan," she said.

"True enough."

"So is Ha'ole a derogatory term or not?"

"It depends on the speaker's intentions and intonations. The way locals speak—they call that language *pigeon*—you have to use all your senses to know the real meaning."

"How did it come to mean people who don't breathe deeply?"

"Back in the days of Captain Cook, foreigners didn't know how to use the 'honi,' which is the way we greet and kiss by touching nose-to-nose and inhaling and sharing each other's breaths. So the foreigners were described as *breathless.*"

"Can a person learn how not to be a ha'ole?"

Kaikoa laughed, "If you learn and respect the local ways, you get respect back. Then if the island adopts you— after about three or four years—you become *Kama'aina.*"

"Three years. I could get a PhD or could become a Kama—"

"*Kama'aina. Kama* means child and *Aina* means land. It translates to child of the land."

"If I had an extra lifetime to spare, that sounds like a very nice thing to do."

"You're always talking about not having time. Ever wonder how come people in Manhattan who pay so much attention to time—and are always racing to be *on time*—have so little of it?"

"Don't you ever feel rushed?" she asked.

"Not really. I mostly feel like I have all the time in the world."

"Wow," April sighed, "I haven't felt that since I was twelve years old."

"That's why they call this Paradise."

"But I love being on time. It takes all the stress out. When you arrive five minutes early to a meeting, you feel in control."

"That's because you are an *on-time* person. You aim to hit a specific spot on the timeline. When you do that, it feels good."

"Yeah," she chided, "You should try it sometime."

"I am an *in-time* person. Which means that for me, whatever is happening *in* the moment may take precedence over a previous or future plan. That's why I'm willing to destroy even a beautiful sand castle. Do you think you can handle that?"

"It would drive me crazy. It just seems to me that being late is disrespectful to the person with whom you made a time commitment. I mean, why agree to meet someone for an eight

AM breakfast meeting if you are not going to be there until after nine?"

"I didn't do that intending to be disrespectful of you. I was just respecting the connection I was having with the waves in that moment. And that connection expanded so much it filled my entire reality."

"Frankly, that just sounds selfish to me."

"I know. That's why I'm trying to widen your perspective about it. In Hawaii we have this understanding; if we say, 'tomorrow we are going to go *holo holo'*—which means go for a joy ride, it doesn't absolutely mean we will go, because the next morning it could be pouring rain. Or the waves could be really going off, you know, big waves, and we would recognize that as a call to the ocean. It's like when we plan, it includes going with the flow, which means to allow the spirit to move you. We like spirit to move us."

"I see. You wouldn't want to miss the call of spirit by being too attached to a previous plan. Or a previous sand castle."

"Exactly. We respect the idea that a deeper reality may unfold, even if we had made other plans."

"I couldn't live like that. If I had a partner who lived in *Now Time*," April made the quote sign with her fingers, "I think I would be too frustrated. I mean, if there's no commitment, what can you count on?"

"You can count on me to honor the moment."

April slid into a silent funk. He had drawn a line in the sand between their two personalities. This was more than just a red flag. This was a neon sign saying, "Get away from this guy right now."

Kaikoa sat quietly for a long time.

Did he sense her dark mood?

"Right now your thoughts are very noisy," he finally said.

"I'm just thinking you and I are very different people. We have different values and we live different lives. We would drive each other crazy. I guess it's good we're having this conversation."

"You look thrilled by it." Kaikoa teased.

April's brow furrowed. She felt like some deep hope he had inspired was gasping for its last breath. She watched an old man in a red kayak slowly paddle into the night waves. He was in no hurry. Maybe there was something about the ocean that made you submit to its rhythm.

"May I make a suggestion?" he asked. "Or have you stopped speaking to me?"

"Go ahead."

"Maybe you don't know what type of person you really are. Maybe you just live in a world that is so ruled by clock time, and you have adjusted so thoroughly, you don't realize it isn't what your spirit truly wants. Perhaps if you surrendered to the power of each moment, you might be amazed to discover *how your Soul likes to tell time.*"

"I would like to. I really would. Honestly, I don't think I can. I'm just not that kind of girl."

"How do you know you're not?"

"How do you know I am?"

"There's really only one way to find out."

"How?"

"Live it."

They walked along the gently lapping shoreline half a mile away from the crowds, soothed in the arms of silence.

Then he stopped and looked at her.

"Have you asked yourself if you would be happier living in Hawaii Time?"

Perhaps it was looking into his eyes, or being this close. Maybe it was the sound of the waves, or the moonlight, or the soothing rhythm of water caressing her ankles; she had the seismic feeling that this moment could shift her destiny.

Her body filled with the sensation of 'yes,' but she couldn't make the word come out of her mouth. Everything in her mind dissolved into a single unanswered question: *Is he going to kiss me?*

Then—a sound intruded—lost in his dreamy eyes she couldn't place it at first.

"It's your cell phone."

"It's my boss. She insists I leave my phone on at all hours."

"We agreed that we were not going to discuss business tonight."

"Yes. And we didn't, right? Here, I'll throw my phone into the ocean." April took the ringing phone, lifted her arm and hurled it toward the waves.

He quickly caught it before it could submerge. "It's not good for the dolphins," he said, and handed it back to her.

By the time she turned off the phone, wiped it off, and gathered her wits, he was gone. As if he'd vanished with the ocean breeze, a gaping hole was all that was left in the space they had shared together.

She couldn't move. Her feet sunk deeper into the wet sand. She had just missed her chance to be swept away. In that moment she hated her boss more than she ever had. Hated that Dana, who woke up at four-thirty AM, had the right to call

April at any hour she pleased. She had been living for the past five years with a personal invasion she had long accepted as normal.

She sat down on the sand and watched the lapping waves, hoping they would calm her nerves. She cursed the cell phone that had so invaded the precious moment that was gone forever.

The torrent of sadness would be unbearable if she allowed herself to be submerged. It was a familiar ache and she forced herself to shift focus to a new view. In a recent Positive Thinking Training at work she had learned to play devil's advocate with the pain. She began looking at the situation from a different point of view. What was the point, of falling for a man who lived in such a different world from hers?   The six hour time zone, and four thousand nine hundred and sixty-eight miles separating them was nothing compared to the distance between their values. He didn't just live in a different time zone—he lived in a completely different relationship to time.

But then the sensation of being near him flooded her. Nothing compared to that.

Like a lab rat in a labyrinth searching for a lost morsel of cheese, her mind scrambled back and forth. *Is his world better than mine?*

Maybe his was more divine. But she was human. She could perhaps enter his world for a weekend taste of paradise, but she could never live there.

And that was that. She had some satisfaction at using her learned mind-skills and pulling herself out of full skid. But the self-congratulatory moment quickly faded. The aching truth was that he was gone—and she wanted him back.

Staring at the Pacific Ocean no longer felt peaceful. She

got up and went looking for her sandals. She looked up and down the beach, but couldn't find the bush where he had hidden them. She was attached to her new Cinderella slippers she had just bought that day. She had to find them. The wish to find them became more and more important, and the chances of doing that became slimmer and slimmer as she walked back and forth, covering the same territory several times.

Maybe he had taken her shoes to punish her. She didn't truly believe that, but just thinking it, made her angry enough to ignore the embarrassment of walking in bare feet through the hotel lobby, up the elevator and down the long floral carpeted hall to her room.

By the time she got to her door, and fumbled with the room card key, the tears had started to fall.

An older, smiling couple walked by, hand-in-hand. They tried to avert their eyes rather than stare too long at a barefoot woman in tears, struggling with her room card key.

The hotel phone inside her room started ringing. Another desperate swipe, and the tiny green light flickered and the lock opened. She raced inside and grabbed the phone.

"This is April," she answered breathlessly.

"This better be good." Her boss's voice pierced her mood.

"It's not," April said, wiping away the tears, hoping Dana couldn't tell she was crying.

A long silence on the other end. April considered hanging up, but her boss was paying for the room she was standing in.

"I guess this means you're going to get busy and figure out how to make it better," Dana said, surprisingly without malice in her voice.

"Yes," April said. She didn't bother trying to make it sound convincing.

"Nothing good will come tonight. We'll talk tomorrow."

"Okay."

"Make sure you answer your phone. I don't do well with voice mail."

The sound on the line went dead. She replaced the phone on the cradle. Well, at least she wouldn't hear her boss's voice for the rest of the night.

Needing more air in her lungs, she threw open the door to the balcony and stepped into the night air. The almost full moon taunted her. It wasn't the same moon they had just gazed upon together. Now the man in the moon was whispering, "*You fool. You lost the most perfect moment. It's buried in time. It's gone now, forever.*"

She went back inside and grabbed her cell phone, ready to toss it over the edge, but instead she put it down on the balcony floor. It could stay there until she checked out.

She sat down on the balcony chair, and listened to the waves. In spite of her recent mind training, she couldn't keep the endless void of sadness away. The maddening chatter in her brain reviewed every moment they had spent together. She dissected each one for errors. Obsessing about her every move and word made her feel as if she was in a mental hall of distorted mirrors. After a long while this Herculean effort at self condemnation wore her out. She gave way to the mercy of sleep.

Chapter Six

The cooing of doves woke her up the next morning. She had slept curled up on the lounge chair on the balcony for ten hours. The mesmerizing sound of the waves had caressed her into a deep, soothing sleep. Usually she had trouble sleeping unless she was lying down in a bed.

She got up slowly, stretching like a sleepy cat. Her motion sent the doves soaring from her balcony. She couldn't remember the last time she had slept straight through for ten hours. In spite of her momentary stiffness, her body felt pretty good.

She had two desires; a shower, and a cappuccino from room service. She ordered a light breakfast, then she stepped into the luxurious shower. But the moment she stepped out of the shower, the inner debate from last night began again. To call or not to call? That was the morning's agonizing question.

She wrapped herself in the hotel's soft robe and

grabbed the matchbook he had given her the night before. Inside he had written BONE YARD and scribbled his number. She dialed quickly before she could chicken out.

A child answered the phone, throwing her completely off her opening line.

"Aloha," the girl's voice said.

"Is your daddy home?"

"No."

The phone fell with a clatter, then another child, a boy, came to the phone and said hello.

"Is your mommy home?" April's heart thumped mercilessly.

"Mommy," the boy called.

April heard a woman's voice in the background. "I'm feeding the baby."

"She's feeding the baby," the boy said.

"I'll call back later." April said and slammed the hotel phone back into its cradle. He was married! Kids and a baby. How dare he flirt with her so brazenly.

She fell onto the mattress, screaming into the pillow— at him.

"I hate you!" She pounded a fist into the pillow. "I hate you!" She tore into the pillow case, ripping a hole in the seam. "You horrible man."

He had played with her heart like it was a squeeze toy. No wonder he disappeared without even so much as a wave goodbye. It all made sense now.

The pain of losing him the night before was nothing compared to this feeling of betrayal. How despicable to not tell her he was married—especially cruel after waking up her heart from years of slumber. She pounded the pillow for several minutes, until the sting of rage dissipated. Slowly it began to dawn on her that she was lucky he had disappeared before things went too far.

A knock at the door interrupted her misery. "Room service," a man's voice said. She tightened the belt on her robe and opened the door. She signed for the food, no longer feeling like eating. The waiter put the tray down on the table, thanked her for the generous tip, and left.

She stared at the artful display, with the glass and steel French coffee press, the purple orchid on the side of the plate next to the croissant and tiny jars of guava, lilikoi and mango jams. She grabbed the flower and ripped savagely at the petals.

An instant later a feeling of horror came over her. How could she treat an innocent flower with such vengeance, especially the same kind of flower whose beauty had touched her yesterday. She picked up each petal, one at a time, and placed them carefully in her hand. She wished there was some way she could make amends for treating it so viciously.

Another knock sounded on the door.

"What is it?" She yelled as if she was in the middle of Manhattan fighting with a cabbie. No reply. The next knock was slower.

She threw open the door.

Kaikoa stood there holding her sandals on a room service tray, complete with a linen napkin.

"You! I hate you! Go away!" She threw the torn petals into his face.

She went to slam the door, but he was faster, and blocked it with his foot.

"I will go away. If you convince me that is what you really want."

"Why didn't you tell me you were married?" she screamed, loud enough for the entire hotel corridor to hear.

He stepped inside and in maddening slow motion, he reverently picked each petal from his shirt. "Because I'm not."

How could he say that with such infuriating calmness?

"Do you live with someone?"

"I live with a lot of someones."

"Whose children are those?"

"Oh." Kaikoa nodded slowly, apparently he was putting it together now. "You called the house."

"Yes, I called the Bone Yard. Several children are very alive there." She crossed her arms firmly across her chest.

"Those are my sister's children. I have no children and I have no wife. I live with my mom, my Tutu, an auntie, a sister and *her* three children. My sister's husband is in the Army."

April kept staring at him. Her hands moved to her hips, eyes like lasers, she was determined to see if he was telling the truth.

He took out his wallet and unfolded a photo copy and presented it to her. It was a picture of his whole family at Christmas. As he spoke he pointed to each person. "That's my mom, my Tutu, Auntie Emma, my sister Maile, her husband Keoki, *their* kids, Keoki junior, and Hoku. That's our dogs Poi and Taro, and our cat Sushi. Those are my four other sisters. Two live on the Big Island, two on Kauai."

April took the picture and studied it. She knew she should apologize but she wasn't ready to let go of her anger.

"Do you have a girlfriend?"

"I have lots of girl *friends*. But no girl friend."

"How come? It seems like everyone on the beach has been your girlfriend at some point. They're probably all swimming in bikinis you bought for them."

"Probably at least a few of those girls bought their own bikinis." He sat down on the bed and assembled the torn petals, as if it were an art project. "Right now, I am unattached," he said.

April took a deep breath and reeled in her emotions.

"Good idea. Breathing is highly recommended."

They exchanged a slow smile.

"What about you?" he said. "Do you come from a large family?"

"You're looking at it."

His confused look made her offer more.

"It's just me. My parents were in a car accident."

"I'm so sorry. When?"

"I was twenty. Nine months later, I got married. Not the best thing to do when you are still grieving."

He nodded. He rearranged the flower petals in a letter "A" pattern and offered them to her. "No brothers or sisters?"

"Only child. Selfish. Work-obsessed. And every other stereotype you can think of."

"I don't think in stereotypes. It numbs the artistic impulses. Anytime you want to borrow a sister or two…"

She smiled. It was a sweet offer.

"May I pour you some coffee or do you have more questions that must be answered first?"

April shook her head no, with a mixture of relief and vulnerability.

"Go sit on the Lanai," he said. "I'll bring out the tray."

"What's a Lanai?"

"It's the word for balcony, Juliet."

April went outside and sat on the comfortable chair that

had been her tear-stained bed. He came out with the tray and put it between them.

"I would have ordered you something," she said sheepishly, "but I wasn't sure if I would ever see you again."

"You weren't sure you wanted to see me again," he said, pouring her coffee.

It was nice to be served. When she saw him looking at her chest, she shyly pulled her robe closed. "Breakfast-in-chair. This is paradise," she said, offering him the second cup that came on the tray.

He accepted the peace offering with a smile. Her smile in return signaled that a thousand tears had washed off to sea.

April sighed happily. "It's the strangest feeling, like I don't want to do anything else. Ever again."

"I call it 'Lanai Duty.' That's when you just sit here and watch the turquoise waves roll in and out, and you realize there isn't anything more perfect than this moment."

They called room service for a second pot of coffee. April tried the four different jams that came with her basket of croissants.

He watched her scoop out the last bit of lilikoi jam from the tiny jar. "Is that one your favorite?"

"First it was the strawberry-guava. Then the lilikoi. But I think my absolute favorite is the mango. It's irresistible."

"My Tutu makes the best mango jam. You'll have to try hers."

"I'd love to." April said, regretting the over-enthusiasm in her voice.

Kaikoa didn't say anything more. She wondered if there was an invisible line that she had crossed when she leapt at the idea of meeting his family. But then, he had suggested it. "I love your painting of the mango. The rich colors. It's magical and real at the same time."

"This isn't you segueing into a business conversation is it?"

"No. I was just saying I love looking at that image. I wasn't trying to—"

"It's okay. We're sitting on a lanai in a beautiful hotel, sipping Kona coffee on your boss's tab. I realize you feel obligated to try."

"Thank you," April said, with a big sigh of relief.

"How come your boss didn't tell you that I turned her down before you came out?"

"When I asked her that, she said she didn't want to prejudice me. I wasn't even supposed to be the one to go, I was supposed to be going to Colorado. Dana switched me with a co-worker, Kristy."

"And we don't like Kristy?" He imitated the exact intonation April used when she said Kristy's name. It made her smile.

"My boss just has this way of making us all very competitive. Which is just one reason why I really should talk to you about the contract."

"I told Dana on the phone I wasn't interested in the deal and she needn't bother to come all the way to Hawaii to talk me out of it."

April sang to the familiar tune; "'Whatever Dana wants, Dana gets.' We sing that at the office. When she's not listening of course."

"Are you ready to talk about why you're really here?"

She felt a jolt. She was relieved when his penetrating eyes finally looked away. He stood up and stretched his arms above his head. "Come on, get dressed. Which, in Hawaii, means your bathing suit, a pareo around your waist, a tank top, and flip flops. I'll take you for a ride around the island. We can't have you leaving here having only seen Waikiki."

She went back inside her room to dress. She liked the fact that he took all the guess work out of stupid things that usually hung her up, like what to wear, what to order, sometimes what to say. If only he could straighten out her heart as easily as these mundane choices.

Moments later she was dressed. Something she could never achieve so quickly in Manhattan. Dressing always plagued her with concern about impressions and power colors, wanting to not over-dress or under-dress for business meetings, how to dress for artist-clients, or their prestige-conscious reps and business managers. She would often debate endlessly with herself over what to wear when meeting someone for the first time. She hated that she put herself through such endless struggles.

Kaikoa came in off the lanai. His eyes said he approved of how she looked.

"Now you look like my island girl."

April blushed. *Did he say "my" island girl?* She felt dizzy, and sat down on the bed to get her bearings. "Whoa. Maybe I had too much of that fabulous Kona coffee."

He came closer, and stood over her protectively. She saw his eyes go to the mattress with the tropical-patterned bedspread.

"How was the bed?" he asked.

"What bed?" April realized how stupid she was sounding, "I mean, I don't know, I slept in the chair on the lanai."

"You probably needed the ocean air. Those negative ions from the ocean clean out your energy field."

"Yeah," was all April could manage. She really wanted to lie down next to him, to feel his body near hers. It was all she wanted—proximity—nothing more.

He looked into her eyes. It was as if he was reading her mind. He put his knee on the bed next to her thigh. It electrified her with anticipation. She could barely breathe.

"We should go now," he said. "Or we will never leave this room."

He walked to the door.

Chapter Seven

The morning sky was perfect, with with high cotton-ball clouds.

"I borrowed my cousin's Sunbird." Kaikoa tilted his head toward the vintage baby-blue convertible. "I didn't think my pick-up truck was the best choice for your first island tour."

The scenery along the southeast corridor of O'ahu along the Kalanianaole Highway coast line was breathtaking. April marveled that a two lane road could be called a highway. The cliffs overlooking the deep blue ocean, the crazy winding turns, it truly was the Hawaii of dreams. He pulled over at Halona Blow Hole Overlook to show her one of his favorite childhood spots.

"It's a lava tube that sucks in the ocean and spits it out. Some days it shoots fifty feet in the air." Just then a huge lofty plume of white water shot so high she felt ocean droplets on her bare arm.

The pure powerful demonstration of Nature was followed by a gust of wind which whipped up from nowhere and made her shiver. Kaikoa moved his body to protect her from the wind and she snuggled next to him.

"This is the beach where they shot the movie *From Here to Eternity*. He pointed to the secluded picture-perfect beach below them, and his arm brushed against her bare shoulder, sending more tiny shudders coursing through her that had nothing to do with the wind.

"You're cold," he said, rubbing her shoulders vigorously.

She nodded. "But I'm okay."

"We'll come back another day with real shoes, and climb down there."

He took her hand and led her back to the car. She took a mental picture so she could remember this scene of romantic tranquility forever.

"When was that movie made?"

"1953. Have you seen it?"

She shook her head.

"Then we'll have to watch it sometime."

She wondered if they were going to have "*a sometime*" or "*another day*" but she didn't want to put those thoughts into words he could hear.

He opened the car door for her and closed it once she was settled.

"I love that you are such a gentleman. I didn't think they made them anymore."

Kaikoa smiled. "Is that your way of saying I'm old fashioned—because I like old movies?"

"It's my way of saying I like everything you do."

He didn't reply. She had to remind herself that direct compliments made him shy.

He turned on the engine, but didn't drive forward.

"April. I have to ask you something."

"What?" The air around them seemed to stop and listen.

"That turtle on your necklace. Do you wear it often?"

"It's my good luck necklace. I only wear it for special times."

"So you knew coming to Hawaii would be a special time."

She paused. Not ready to admit this—even to herself.

"It's funny," she said after a moment. "I almost didn't bring it. I locked my apartment door to leave, and had this impulse to go back and get it."

"Good. Good impulse." He nodded

"Why do you say that?"

"Have you always liked turtles?"

"I love turtles," April said without a moment's hesitation. "It's the only thing I collect. You should see my apartment and my office. It's filled with tiny figurines. I have a whole row of turtles walking across my monitor. First, I just had a couple, but now it's what everybody gives me as a present."

"You ever think about why you are so drawn to turtles?"

She shrugged. "I've just collected them since I was a little girl. Turtles are my symbol."

"You think about why?"

"Dunno. I like that they never go backwards. They just keep moving ahead."

He seemed genuinely happy with her answer. "Have

95

you ever met a real one?"

"No, but I've always wanted to. You don't get much opportunity for close encounters in Manhattan."

"You will now. We're going to have a visit with the real thing." He shifted into drive. "We're going to have a talk with the turtles."

* * *

Known as the "surfing capital of the world," Oahu's North Shore spans from La'ie to Ka'ena Point. He drove expertly through the winding, twisting roads as if he knew them intimately. It was like being in a whole new universe.

"Most tourists don't even make it out this far," he said.

"I can't imagine coming all this way and missing this," April exclaimed, as they drove through the famous red dirt land of the former pineapple fields, and saw the ocean looming ahead.

When he got past the historic town of Haleiwa and got close to an unmarked turn, he told her to close her eyes.

"I don't want the whole world knowing my secret beach," he said as he turned down the narrow gravel road. "This is one of the spots where the Turtles hang out."

April nodded. This was no ordinary sightseeing stop. She had never seen a wild sea turtle, and her pulse quickened, knowing she was about to see one.

"Turtles are my family's Aumaukua. Aumaukua are spirit guides who protect and watch over a family," he said. "We talk to them. Listen to them when we need advice."

She had no idea what it meant to talk to an Aumauakua. She just hoped she wouldn't mess it up.

The car slowed and she heard the wheels crunching over gravel. Then it stopped.

"You can open your eyes now," he said. He grabbed a woven beach mat out of the trunk, and didn't say another word, as they walked through a path of trees to a pristine beach. The waves lapped gently. No one else was here.

She quietly let him lead without having to have all the "Why" and "How" answers to what was going on. He unrolled the woven mat and laid it on the sand. He took off his Tee shirt and set his flip flops on top to keep the light mat from blowing away. She unwrapped her pareo and anchored it on the mat with her sandal. It was only yesterday that she was almost too shy to let him see her in her bathing suit. Today it seemed easy and natural. She followed him down to the water's edge.

He stared for a very long time at the water.

"There they are," he said.

She looked, but saw only waves and ocean. She patiently continued to gaze at the spot where he was pointing. Gradually, she could make out some moving brown shapes in the distance.

"The Hawaiian word for turtle is honu," he said.

Honu, Honu, Honu. She repeated the word to herself many times to burn it into her mind. She looked at him. His eyes were closed.

"Are you praying?" she asked.

"I'm asking for permission."

"From the honu?"

"Yes. After all, it's their house, we're just visitors."

"What did they say?

"Come in."

April held back a smile. She wanted to believe, but

97

wasn't quite there yet.

"How do you hear them? I mean do you hear the words in your head? Or?"

"They're not super chatty. It's like a feeling, a knowing, I can feel their answer. Kind of like the way the wind whispers over you. Ready?"

"Yes," April said without knowing what she was agreeing to. "What do I do?"

"Just enter slowly and float."

"Okay." She followed him into the water. He glided in with a slow grace that reminded her of a Qi Gong Master. Every motion was in sync with the waves, a dance with the rhythms of the ocean.

He lay back into a floating position. She copied him, but unlike him, she had no clue what was going on. The ocean moved her gently, massaging her body. It was like getting a chiropractic water-adjustment with the ocean lining up all the vertebrae. She forgot about worry, she forgot about the future, she forgot about time. She drifted into a timeless time.

She didn't know how long it had been but when she looked over at Kaikoa she saw they had drifted apart by about twenty yards. Just when she turned she saw a turtle approach him very close and then it swam underneath him. He didn't move, just let the waves carry him on the liquid rise and fall. She treaded water, watching the amazing sight of the turtle swimming so close and then underneath him. The turtle did this three times. This mysterious dance between them, with the turtle leading, was extraordinary.

But it made her nervous to be so far from Kaikoa and she started to swim back to shore. The exertion of the swim felt good. She lay down on the woven mat on the soft sand and soon drifted into the kind of delicious sleep that only happens on sweet, gentle, quiet beaches.

She didn't know how long she had drifted off, but when she awoke he was sitting next to her. His hair and body were still wet.

"How did it go?" she asked.

"Very well." He smiled, leaned back on an elbow and looked at her.

"Are you going to tell me or is it a secret Aumuakua communication?"

"They told me to bring you to the Bone Yard for dinner tonight."

April rolled onto her side to look into his eyes.

"Does this mean I'm meeting the family?"

"Ah, huh." And with that he lay onto his back and closed his eyes.

After a moment she poked him.

"Does this mean—" She couldn't bring herself to say it out loud.

"It means now is the moment where you decide if you want your whole life to change."

She sat up straight and stared at him.

"Is this—was that some kind of proposal?"

He sat up and faced her.

"This is me saying 'Here we are.' He drew a line in the sand with a stick. At the end he made the line fork in two directions. "We're past the point of pretending you are here on business and trying to talk me into a deal I've already said no to. We are at a choice point."

April stared at the line drawing in the sand. Her heart beat faster. "Are you saying, you would choose me?"

"I am saying I have already chosen. Now you have to choose."

"But you don't even know me."

"That's why I wanted to check with the Honu."

April's brain spun. *This is moving too fast.* Her body felt magnetized by him, but she didn't know if she should trust that. She had never gotten that right before, and she had never met a man who was that sure about her.

"But you live in Hawaii, and I have this great job in New York. Would you consider moving to New York?"

"No."

"Wow. Take your time thinking about it."

"I have. I'm an Island Boy. I can't live without the ocean. And—well, you'll meet the family."

"Let me get this straight. Are you saying that if I give up my New York life, and my apartment, and my job and my cat and move to Hawaii, we'd be like . . . together?"

"Bring your cat."

He was so sure of all this. April laughed. "Isn't that a bit old-fashioned? The girl giving up her entire life and career to live with the Island Boy?"

"*Old fashioned* implies that modern times are better than olden times. I'm not sure that's true. Why not choose the best aspects of each and just live in the *best of times*?"

"See? We can't even agree on how we relate to time. You are like a wave—and I'm like a mountain. How are we going to work that out?"

Kaikoa smiled at the analogy. He pointed to the mountain in the distance, then to the ocean. "The mountain and the ocean seem to have worked it out being near each other for thousands of years."

"It's easy for a mountain. But I can't just change my relationship to time. It's how I live my life. It's who I am."

"April, are you happy in your modern time in New York?"

Her mouth moved but words didn't follow at first. "I've worked hard. I have a great job. I'm on a career path. I have an apartment four blocks from the subway."

"Do you have a nice view?"

"If you consider the apartment building across the street a nice view. But there is a tree on my block." April wasn't even convincing herself.

"How big is your apartment?"

"It's a studio. But it's an older building and fairly quiet and it's only three flights up. But the point is my whole career is in New York. I can't just give up my whole life. We haven't even kissed. How do you know we would—you know—be good."

"I know."

"You know as in 'you know what I mean?' Or 'you know' as in 'knowing we would be—you know.'" She babbled. "Maybe we should just have an affair. I mean, I guess it's not an affair since neither one of us is married."

"Would that convince you?"

April had to think for a moment but she was spared having to say yes out loud.

"I'm certain I could convince you that way," he said. "But that's not how I want to do it."

"How do you want to do it?"

"I want your heart to make the decision."

"Are you saying you don't want to sleep with me?" Getting mad at him was easier than facing her own panic.

"I want to sleep with you more than you can imagine."

"Really?" was all April could say. Her heart was thumping out of her chest.

"Really," he said. "But if we are going to choose to be together, I want us to choose from a different kind of knowing."

Chapter Eight

They left the car with the valet in front of the hotel and walked across Kalakaua Avenue to Waikiki Beach. Standing there she understood the reason that over four million tourists come here each year. There is something about this former playground for royalty that sweeps you away. Kaikoa sat down on a bench to watch the waves as the sun dropped lower in the sky.

"I'll be quick," she said. "I just want to jump in the shower and put on my dress."

"Take your time. I'm not going anywhere."

"Okay," April said. "I will." Kaikoa didn't see her smile. He seemed mesmerized by the sunset waves, and watching the surfers paddling out.

She grinned as she rode the elevator to her floor. Strangers smiled back and said "Aloha." There were definitely some nice advantages to being with somebody who wasn't worried about time. It was different not to rush. Unfamiliar. She was not only in another time zone, but learning how to relate to time differently.

Inside her hotel room her cell phone glared at her. Taunting her. She should call her boss. It was midnight in New York but she could leave a voice mail. Besides, if she didn't check in, Dana would just hound her at all the wrong times.

She rehearsed a possible short message. "Things going well.Communication flowing. Hope to address deal terms tomorrow." Hopefully that was sufficiently positive, but still vague enough to be remotely possible. She hit her boss's name and on the second ring, a sleepy Dana answered.

"Tell me you're close to a deal memo."

"Not really," April said, suddenly opting for the truth.

Dana was silent for a long moment. Then said, "What's your game plan?"

"I'm having dinner with him tonight."

"Take him someplace expensive."

"Actually, we're—"

"*We're* what?"

"Going to the Bone Yard."

"The what?"

"It's an old Chinese Cemetery."

"Who puts a restaurant in a cemetery?"

"It's where his family lives. For three generations—"

"April. What exactly is going on here?"

"I don't know."

Dana was silent again. Through five thousand miles of fiber optic phone lines, April imagined the thoughts burning in her boss's mind.

"Whatever is going on, is there any chance it might lead to a signed deal in the near future?"Dana's voice was controlled but clearly angry.

"I don't know," April mumbled.

"Tell me something you *do* know."

"I know I am having dinner with him."

Dana sighed. "You will come home with a signed contract. If you care about your job."

"You know how hard I work. You know how much I—"

"If this trip turns out to be a *joy ride*, I'll consider deducting it from your paycheck."

April swallowed hard. Dana did not make idle threats. Generally, what she said, she did. April looked around the Business Class hotel room. Moderate by resort standards, but still close to two hundred dollars a night. The ocean view made the room look suddenly extravagant. And a pile of receipts, and boarding pass stubs and the new dress hanging in the closet, reminded her nothing was free.

"I understand." April managed.

"I hope you do." Dana hung up.

April stared at the phone. Part of her wished she hadn't made the call, but it would have been on her mind and dishonest to pretend she was getting somewhere with this business deal. It was a relief to have been truthful about her lack of progress. Even though it was scary to think about having to pay for this trip, she refused to give into the fear. As Kaikoa might say, "Why worry about something that might happen in the future?" She pushed the tug of panic out of her mind. She just wanted to indulge the compelling pull of the evening ahead of her. Perhaps Kaikoa's "be in the moment" magic had cast a spell on her.

She stepped into the shower and said his name out loud to feel it on her lips.

* * *

The Bone Yard was tucked away deep in the lush Manoa Valley. Surrounded by green mountain ridges, it appeared as a part of town less touched by time. They turned past the residential area into a tree secluded grove, and up ahead was the two-hundred year-old cemetery. April did not mention her phone call with her boss. *Why bring that polluted energy into the sweetness weaving all around us?*

"Did you tell your family you were bringing me over?"

"The Honu probably told them."

April checked his face to see if he was being serious. He was.

The historic plantation style house emerged up ahead. It looked as if it had withstood the world for a very long time. Tilting ever so slightly, it rested somewhere between its former Chinese elegance and the inevitable dilapidation of being so old.

As they drove up the S curved driveway, two Labradors came bounding up. They barked in greeting and jumped up to meet Kaikoa.

He did his best to give them equal attention.

"How long have you been gone? Or is this the daily greeting?"

"Any absence over two hours gets the full on slobber."

"Poi, Taro, go greet our guest," Kaikoa said, and as if the dogs understood English, they obeyed, and romped over to April. "Nicely," Kaikoa admonished and they restrained themselves mid-leap and sat by her feet, looking up adoringly, so she could pet them, which she did with total enthusiasm. Instantly they were on their backs, showing soft bellies. She

106

knelt down next to them, doing her best to reach all their favorite spots.

"They'll keep you here all night. We'll have to bring *you* a bowl of food and water. Come on, ladies."

Kaikoa started walking toward the house, the dogs trotting at his side. April stood up and smoothed out her dress. She was glad he had taken her back to the hotel so she could wear her pretty new Hawaiian dress, but a trickle of sweat down her neck reminded her how nervous she was about meeting his family.

Ukulele music sounded from inside the house, which was surrounded by tropical trees with huge leaves and graceful Red Ginger plants.

"Uncle's home," a little girl's voice called. She came running out the screen door, and in one smooth move, leapt into Kaikoa's arms.

"Aloha, Leilani," the girl said to April.

"Hoku, say hi to April."

"Hello, Hoku," April said, trying not to be rattled by being called by another woman's name.

Then a young barefoot boy came bounding out. "Uncle, I caught this really gnarly wave. It was probably like six feet." He stretched his arms wide. "Well, maybe not six, but almost." He demonstrated the kinetic balance of surfing a huge wave. I rode it all by myself for like forever."

Kaikoa nodded. "I didn't hear about any six footers today. You sure it wasn't maybe two?"

The boy's face showed he had been caught in the exaggeration.

"Did you say hello to our guest?"

"Aloha, Leilani," Keoki, Jr. said. He seemed

disappointed that his story didn't get a better reception.

"Her name is Mohala," the little girl offered.

"That's the Hawaiian word for the month of April," Kaikoa said. April was getting resigned to the fact that people seemed to want to call her by something other than her own name.

"April. This is Hoku and Keoki."

"Nice to meet you. How old are you?"

"I'm eight. And she's six," Keoki offered.

"Six and a quarter. Do you want to see my room?"

"Let's let April come in the door first and meet everyone. Then she can see your room."

Keoki ran to hold open the screen door which still had the original wood, patched many times. The screens in the various sections of the door didn't match.

"This isn't really our front door," Keoki said.

April walked into a room that was bigger than her whole apartment. There were three industrial sinks, two mismatched refrigerators, one painted red and the other blue, and an enormous restaurant style freezer. An assortment of magnets and children's drawings covered their doors. The *stove* was homemade, with bricks, gas pipes and eight burners. The cupboards were well stocked with pots and pans in all sizes, and there was enough counter space to cook for a battalion. A large round homemade monkey pod wooden table stood in the middle of the room.

Although nothing matched, it was clear that this family loved to cook and that this room was the heart of the house. Whatever was bubbling on the stove smelled delicious.

Hoku took April's hand to show her, "All the pictures on the *red* refrigerator are by me. And the ones on the *blue* one are by Keoki."

"A family of artists," April said as she looked with admiration.

"Ah, huh." Hoku nodded proudly. "These ones on the freezer are from other people who came to dinner and stuff. There's not really much room left but if you want to paint something, we could move things around."

"Thank you," April said, already falling for Hoku's charm.

The swinging doors of the walk-in cupboard opened. A large woman in a pink muumuu emerged. She carried the largest jar of mayonnaise that April had ever seen. Her friends in New York were afraid of mayonnaise, as if it would create instant fat just by looking at it.

"Is that Leilani?" the woman beamed, staring in April's general direction.

"It's Mohala," the kids chimed in.

"The Honu said Leilani was coming for a visit," Tutu said.

"Tutu is blind," Hoku said, and led April over to her.

"Tutu is their great-grandmother," Kaikoa said.

The large woman gave April a warm hug, as if she was long lost family.

Then Kaikoa's mom emerged from the walk-in cupboard.

"This is my Emma, my mom. Mom, this is April."

Emma put down the huge container of Shoyu sauce she carried and gave April a good look before giving her the same warm hug.

"She looks kind of thin, eh?" his mom said.

Kaikoa shook his head. "She's not thin. She lives in

109

Manhattan."

Everyone nodded their heads as if this somehow explained everything.

"They don't eat in Manhattan?" Hoku asked.

"They talk business while they eat. So they don't get much food in their mouth," Kaikoa quipped.

"Do they have good surfing in Manhattan?" Keoki asked.

"Only on the web," April said.

Emma smiled at her effort at humor.

Kaikoa's sister, Maile, walked in, a ten-month old baby in her arms.

"This is my *sister,* Maile, and *her* baby, Emma." Kaikoa said.

"So nice to meet you all," April said. "Thank you for having me to dinner. I would have brought something but I'm staying at a hotel." She wished she had made Kaikoa stop and pick up something from a store. Everyone was staring in her general direction. She felt like an exotic alien.

"No worries. We'll put you to work," his sister Maile said.

"I have no problem making you work for your supper," his mom added. "Okay, boys, go to the garden. I need lettuce, cucumber, basil, tomatoes and peppers."

"By the time I get back, they'll know more about you than I do," Kaikoa whispered. Then he and Keoki took off for the garden in back.

"What can I do to help?" April asked. She hoped it would be something easy.

"What are you good at?" Hoku said with the kind of directness that little girls can get away with.

"Umm. Nothing really." April felt overdressed in this kitchen. "I can wash dishes."

Tutu and Emma laughed heartily and Hoku joined in.

"I didn't think there was any room in Kaikoa's bed," Tutu whispered to Maile. Maile gave Tutu a poke, and April pretended she hadn't heard.

"You know what this is?" Kaikoa's mom, Emma, held up a peeler.

"Of course," April said. "You use that to hammer nails in the wall."

Everyone laughed. April was relieved that at least it was easy to entertain them.

"She's funny," Tutu said approvingly. "Not like that other one."

* * *

The open air lanai had three tables lined up together and covered with colorful but mismatched vinyl tablecloths. Oil lamps lit the screened-in patio. The children had set the table for twelve. Each setting had a plate with different tropical flower designs. None of the glasses matched either, because, as Hoku explained, "That's so everybody knows whose glass is theirs." The green Ti leaves and red ginger made the whole presentation charming. There were homemade candles everywhere. April had a flash of concern for the open flames, with all the old wood that held this house together.

She didn't have to wonder for very long who the extra table settings were for, because just as they had taken hands to say grace, the family next door, the Nehoa's and their three hungry teenage kids, arrived. It was a relief to have the attention diverted from her.

It had been fun earlier during the dinner preparation, hearing the women in Kaikoa's family gossip about the Nehoa family next door, so April already knew that the husband had once again lost his job. She was trying to match the other stories she had just heard with the faces now seated at the table. It was a guilty pleasure to have *inside* information.

Kaikoa's sister Maile sat next to April during dinner and whispered in her ear. "That's the one who has three boyfriends."

"Right. One Filipino, one Samoan, one Japanese," April whispered back. "She's so beautiful. It's amazing she only has three."

"And that's the one that's learning French because she met a boy online who lives in Paris."

"And the brother is the boy you said was washing cars to secretly pay for ballroom dance lessons."

Maile nodded her approval of April's attention to detail. April smiled back, feeling like an insider already.

Several times during dinner she found herself fleetingly linking eyes with Kaikoa. It was like being in high school and having a secret crush.

She was glad that she was seated next to Kaikoa's sister Maile, because Maile helped her navigate through the exotic local foods. The smooth long *glass noodles* looked very strange, and she was surprised to discover they were delicious. It was one of the first dishes to disappear from the big serving bowls. The lomi-lomi salad with salmon bits was not at all what she expected. It had a tangy coolness on the tongue. The shredded smoked Kalua pig was tender and juicy.

There was so much delicious food. Even the white rice

seemed fluffier than anything she had had before. "How do you get the rice so soft?" she asked.

"Tutu's secret recipe," Keoki said. "She's won awards and stuff and she won't tell anybody the secret."

"She prays into the water. Then she uses the healing water for the rice," Maile whispered to April. "Everyone says it's the best rice."

Tutu nodded her head proudly.

"That's how come all the neighbors stop by our house for dinner," Kaikoa said.

The husband looked a little sheepish. "We'd be happy to entertain after dinner, for your guest."

"Of course. You know you're always welcome here." Kaikoa's mom wagged a finger at her son.

"Mahalo, Tutu, Auntie Emma. Everything is so *ono*. We are very grateful," Mrs. Nehoa, the neighbor mom said. "You just say the word and the kids will help with any house project."

April noticed that the Nehoa kids nodded gratefully. This was definitely a different world, where teenagers wanted to give something back.

After so much dinner, two desserts—chocolate Haupia Pie, and Bread Pudding—were carried to the lanai table. And the neighbors had brought brightly colored mochi for dessert— the Japanese glutinous rice sweet treat that the kids inhaled. Saying 'no thank you' to anything was clearly not an option.

When everyone was finished eating, April was impressed that the children began clearing the table without being asked. The kids had it down to a routine. Hoku gathered the silverware and put it on a tray. Keoki gathered plates, and the neighbor kids helped carry trays back to the kitchen.

Once everything was in the kitchen, everyone helped clean up. The three sinks made sense now.

"This sink is for silverware and glasses," Hoku said. "This one is for plates."

"And this one is for the really yucky pots and pans," Keoki added, disappointed with the station that he and Kaikoa were assigned.

"I see. You guys are geniuses at making everything squeaky clean," April said, and Keoki smiled proudly.

"Hey, I do all the scrubbing," Kaikoa answered in his imitation of an eight-year-old voice. "He just dries and hands them over to Mom."

The feeling of cooperation was palpable and everyone had a task. Tutu held the baby, and the neighbors dried and put dishes away, while Mr. Nehoa kept a run of jokes going, like the former cruise director MC he had been. With this teamwork, within twenty minutes everything was washed, dried and put away.

With playful pomp, Tutu announced, "Okay, everyone to the Grand Parlor."

They moved into the living room, which was big enough to hold the six mismatched sofas arranged in a semi-circle. Everyone settled in to the comfy, well-worn, large-size seating. The fabric of each piece had a different tropical pattern, but the total homey effect had a coherent style all its own. The old style gas lights gave a warm glow that made everything look special.

"The reason why nothing matches is that people always give us furniture when they move," Emma said.

"Or to pay for all those suppers," Kaikoa whispered, as he led April to his favorite couch. When everyone was seated, the candlelight concert began.

Whatever gossip April had been told disappeared from her mind when she heard the neighbor family perform. The father and son played ukulele, and the mother and two daughters sang like angels. The mother held the last beautiful high note for what seemed an eternity, without running out of breath. They played old Hawaiian favorites that Tutu requested, and she even got up and danced a traditional hula for one soulful tune called "Hanalei Moon."

Then Kaikoa's mother, Emma, and his sister, Maile, got up to dance a Hula together. Maile was about to hand over the baby to Tutu, but April reached out to hold her. Baby Emma took to her instantly, smiling to April's baby-play faces and sounds. When April looked up, she saw that everyone was quiet and watching her, as if she was now the one performing.

"What?" April asked Kaikoa, wondering why she was suddenly the center of attention. Kaikoa just smiled. His mother looked at him and nodded. Had she just passed some kind of unspoken test?

The music began again and the attention moved from her. Emma and Maile danced a graceful hula, and when it was over Maile made no effort to take the baby away from April.

Then Hoku and Keoki performed together, which made everyone laugh and applaud—as Keoki ended the dance with some fancy hip-hop moves of his own.

"You should audition for *So You Think You Can Dance*," April said, but Keoki just gave her a blank stare.

"We don't have a TV," Maile said.

"We only have electricity in the kitchen," Kaikoa added. "From the generator. And no, we don't have wi-fi."

"Oh," April said, feeling suddenly out of sync with

everyone. "Sorry."

"Don't be sorry. We like it this way. Can you feel how peaceful it is here without all that electricity buzzing through your brain?"

"It is very soothing here," April agreed. Everyone smiled and nodded their appreciation that she could sense this.

Kaikoa's mom saw the tender looks and glances that were passing between her son and April. "Go ahead, son, sing for her," his mom said.

Kaikoa hesitated, but everyone cheered him on so he couldn't refuse. He slowly stood and took the ukulele the neighbor's son handed him. He had a simple, unadorned playing style, but his voice was rich and resonant as he sang a mesmerizing old song in Hawaiian called "Ka Wai Lehua," about the rain returning to the sea.

And in that moment April knew she wanted to hear that voice every day.

Chapter Nine

After a magical night of songs, the neighbors left. April helped Maile put the kids to bed.

"You're not really leaving Hawaii tomorrow, Auntie April," Hoku said, hanging onto her with all of her six-year-old force.

"Maybe I can come back some day," April said, as her heart gave a tug.

"If you just stay, then you don't have to come back," Keoki chimed in.

"Auntie April has a whole different life in New York," Maile said.

April nodded, grateful to be understood. She looked up and saw Kaikoa standing in the doorway watching them.

"Let go of Auntie April. It's time for dreams," Kaikoa said.

"Are you going to dream with Auntie now?" Hoku

asked.

April wondered why that got a chuckle from the grownups.

"We're going to take a walk in the garden," Kaikoa answered.

"But it's dark. How's she supposed to see anything?"

"There's a full moon tonight. There are things you can see in the moonlight that you never see during the day."

"Uncle, are you going to kiss Auntie in the moonlight?" Keoki asked.

Everyone burst into giggles. April turned several shades of red.

"I don't know. But if I do, you will be the second person to know."

"What about me?" Hoku demanded.

"You'll be third."

Hoku seemed satisfied with that, and let go of April.

"You guys better hurry up. The moon doesn't stay up forever," Hoku announced. She lay back down under her covers.

April blew kisses to the children and she and Kaikoa left.

She fell silent as they walked to the garden. She sensed that tonight was about Kaikoa showing her—without words— why he couldn't just pack up his paints and move to Manhattan.

Kaikoa took her hand and led her to the hill at the top of the cemetery. His touch was firm and alive. Currents of warm energy passed from his hand to hers communicating more than words could say.

When they got to the top, she looked around. It was

strange, beautiful and sacred. Many of the tombstones were over a hundred years old and some had tilted with time. Even the whispers in the wind sounded older here.

She had a flash of wondering if her parents were watching her in this moment. But she pushed this thought away. She wasn't ready to cross into that realm of possibility.

The Chinese Mausoleum at the top was ornate enough to hold an Emperor. April wondered about the man inside. *Had he been a kind, or stern person? Had he married for love, or duty? Were his children buried with him?*

The line between this world and the next felt very thin at the top of this hill, and the full moon made everything even more magical.

Kaikoa finally broke the silence. "So how was your audition for the family?"

"They surprised me. I thought they were going to grill me on everything from my high school report card to my taxes. But they really only asked me three questions."

"What were they?"

"Did I like Hawaii? Why was I leaving? And how did I like swimming with the turtles?"

"They only asked you three questions out loud. The rest was just observing you and sensing who you are."

"How come everybody got so quiet when I was holding the baby?"

"They were just seeing if you had the 'mommy-juice.'"

April thought about that. She was curious. "So, do I have it?"

"You've got it."

April smiled. The flood of how good she felt surprised her. But then just about everything that happened around

Kaikoa felt good. And surprising.

He came closer to her, touched his forehead to hers, and inhaled her scent. His eyes were closed. His proximity just made her want more of everything from him but he stood back and sighed. Then he opened his eyes and looked into hers.

"That is the Honi," he said. "It's the ancient kiss of Hawaii."

She could feel his energy mingling with hers, and the sublime sensation made her unsure where his body ended and hers began. She could bear it no longer. "Is this the moment where you kiss me? In present time?"

"Yes."

And his hungry lips found hers.

* * *

It was nearly midnight when he drove the convertible to the front of her hotel. There was no way that she was ready for this perfect night to end. A gentle drizzle began. He looked up at the sky, inviting the mist to touch his cheeks.

"That's the Goddess Pele washing her face," he said.

Did he remember that she was leaving tomorrow afternoon? His smoky brown eyes revealed nothing. "Now what?" she said.

"Now you get some sleep. Ask the *Honu* for an answer in your dreams."

"I can't sleep. We need to talk more. I mean, there's so much to figure out."

"It's *too* much to figure out. That's why you need to ask the Turtles to send you a dream. Ask for a symbol that will explain everything."

April sighed. As much as she had loved turtles all her life, she was not optimistic about the *Honu* giving her answers in her dream to the biggest decision in her life.

"Would you come upstairs with me?"

Kaikoa turned and looked into her eyes.

"I need to give you a copy of the contract. I can't go back to New York and tell my boss I never gave you the contract. Even if you're not going to sign it, would you do me a favor and please at least read it—so I can honestly say I tried to do my job?"

"If it will make you feel better, I will read it. But it might take me a week to read twenty-eight pages of legalese."

"Thank you. It's really important to me that I did the best I could. And my boss may—or may not—pay for this trip."

"She would do that?"

"That's what she said."

"Go and get it. I'll wait here."

"I wish you'd come up with me."

Kaikoa looked up at the full moon as if there was an answer there.

"Not a good idea."

The pang of his restraint hit her like a sucker punch. Embarrassed and exposed for having made such a bold request —and be rejected, turned her into a raging stallion. "Forget I asked." She yelled and swung the door open. "Why should you care if you'll never see me again?" She slammed it shut. "Let's spare us both the charade of pretending I'm good at my job." She stalked toward the front door.

He did nothing to deter her on her sudden streak of irrational fury.

* * *

Storming through the lobby, she saw a young couple kissing by the balcony.

I wonder how many other people had kissed for the first time tonight under this Hawaiian full moon. What were they doing right now? Declaring their love? Making plans for the future? Making love? When she got inside the elevator and realized she couldn't call him on his nonexistent cell phone, a torrent of regret hit her. *Why did I even say that about being good at my job? He must be totally confused about why I invited him upstairs.* She had lashed out like a crazy woman—crazy from all this newly awakened desire. It had taken a lot of guts to make such a bold move, and now it seemed so foolish. She'd practically said *come upstairs and make love to me.*

And now she was riding the elevator alone.

And he was driving home to the Bone Yard in a full moon.

Feeling heavier with each step, she walked along the corridor to her room. She was leaving tomorrow afternoon and they hadn't made any plans. He didn't even know what time she was leaving for the airport. Even if they had made a plan, could she trust him to keep it? Maybe the waves would be *going off* and he would leave her standing there with her suitcase in the hotel lobby like a love struck idiot.

Her emotions were hijacking her and she could do nothing to stop the crash. The ride was moving too quickly. *I must be a lunatic to slam the car door—not even saying goodbye—to a man I just kissed under the full moon.*

He wasn't just *a* man. He wasn't just *any* man. He was

the man who had touched her so intimately—without even touch. She needed to know him in that way. To know if this was just a fanciful, powerful attraction or if he was someone she could trust at the deepest level of connection.

Judging by her recent explosion, maybe he was right. Maybe rushing into sex would just wreak greater havoc with her emotions and make it harder to see clearly. Maybe she was just under the spell of the moon

Watching the elevator numbers slowly climb, all she wanted to do was go back down. But after her rude exit, he would surely be gone. And it was too late to call his house and wake everyone. The quaint idea of the whole family sharing one phone line didn't feel very good right now.

She opened the door of room 936 and flopped down on her bed. She was too mad at herself to sleep. What horrible, rotten, wild-haired troll inside of her made her ruin such a fairy-tale evening?

She got up and retrieved her cell phone from the lanai and stared at this electronic lifeline with eight unread text messages from her boss. It snapped her back to reality. Who was she kidding? She and Kaikoa lived in not only totally different time zones—but totally different time-realities. Hawaii Time, he had called it. *I could never live in his moment-to-moment world.*

She should take a taxi to the airport right now and put herself out of her misery. She did a search on her phone and found a flight back to New York at six AM. It was fully booked. She called the airline and there were only two people on stand-by, so she added her name to the list. Although she was scheduled to leave the next night on the red-eye, leaving eighteen hours earlier made sense to her tormented brain. It was one AM now. That left just a few hours to endure paradise. She should probably stay up so she would sleep on the plane.

She might as well call Dana and tell her she had washed up with the contract. It was six AM in New York. She dialed and Dana answered, without even a polite hello.

"Is it good news?"

"No." It wouldn't help to explain.

"You're on the clock here. Is it going to *become* good news?"

"No. I'm on stand-by for the morning flight."

Dana was quiet. The pulse in April's head was throbbing.

"Update me if you get on board."

"Yes, M'am." April knew the polite military style of communication worked well with her boss. She used it sparingly, but it always seemed to calm her down.

As usual, the line went dead.

April went back inside the room and stuffed everything into her suitcase—not thinking about a traveling outfit. She hadn't brought much and she was a fast packer even when she wasn't upset. Fifteen minutes later she was done.

Maybe it was for the best to end like this. If they couldn't live in the same reality, it was a good thing they never made love. Perhaps he knew that, and being a gentleman he was sparing her heart from the inevitable searing pain of separation after such closeness.

But thinking about him protecting her—even protecting her from the loss of his touch—drew her heart to him like a magnet. *Maybe I was too timid. I should have seduced him and gone for one night of perfect abandonment.* Wondering how it would have been to be naked in his arms was the worst form of torture.

She put her suitcase by the door and looked at her watch. She wondered if the bar downstairs was still open. She was still dressed and she needed a drink. She smoothed back her hair and put on lipstick for the first time since the morning she had arrived.

Part of her felt crazy even thinking about going out this late. Nothing good could come from going out with a hungry heart at one in the morning.

But the quiet of the room echoed with reminders of how foolish she had just been. Even the orchid which she had saved from their first breakfast together still looked miraculously fresh, and seemed to be taunting her. The petals of the second one that she had torn apart were still in a little glass dish. She had to get out of there. To forget everything for awhile. One of the hotel's fabulous Mai Tai's would be the perfect prescription to wash away her burning thoughts.

She took a deep breath and tore open the door.

And there he was.

"Kaikoa," she gasped. Was he real or part of her desperate imagination?

"Where are you going in your bright red lipstick?"

He sounded angry. This was a side of him she hadn't seen.

"I was told you can't leave Hawaii without having had at least three Mai Tai's. I've only had one and—"

Kaikoa saw her suitcase by the door. "Give me the contract."

"Forget it. We don't have to pretend you want to—"

He grabbed her suitcase and put it outside the door and closed it. She stared aghast.

"The contract."

She grabbed it from the dresser and handed it to him. He folded it irreverently and stuck it in his pocket. Her heart skipped a beat—he was still inside the door—*and her suitcase was outside*. Her brain spun. "Can we talk?"

He nodded. Waited for her to go on.

"I'm sorry I acted like—" she couldn't finish.

"Like someone who's confused."

"Yes. I just don't know if we—" All the words that were forming in her brain seemed twisted.

"Now you understand how I feel." he said. "How can I move even one inch forward with you when you're not sure?"

It was as if he had drawn another line in the sand. She had to cross it. Now or never.

"Yesterday morning you couldn't take off your pareo in front of me."

"That was yesterday."

"I am not the rip-off-the-pareo kind of guy. I have to know it's really what you want. We're like turtles. We can't go backward with each other."

April's heart leapt. He hadn't moved an inch closer from the doorway. She hesitated a moment. "What if this is how I find out?" April said. She lifted her dress above her head and flung it away. She stood before him in her new French black lace panties and bra.

His eyes wandered over every curve.

An unexplored power awakened in her and she boldly struck a lingerie model pose.

"Purrfect" His voice was like exotic tea, steeped in sensation. His lips parted, as if to taste her potential.

Oh, to hold this moment forever. The fierce connection

created a current between them. All she wanted was to play in this flow of energy and find out where it would lead. Feeling the heat of his gaze, she breathlessly waited for his next move.

"I can't wait." He said without taking his eyes off her. "But you will."

He stepped past her and took the fluffy white hotel robe off the hook.

"What are you doing?"

"I know you're going to be angry at me but I can't let you and your red lips go anywhere."

It hit her like hot oil that he wasn't going to stay. He was taking all her clothes and leaving.

"I'll be back in the morning to get you." He turned to leave.

She stopped him at the door. "Wait. I don't want you to leave me tonight."

"It's not just about tonight. When you say, "Don't *ever* leave me'—that's when I'll stay." He traced a soft hand on her bare skin that made her ache for the certainty of his full touch.

And a moment later he was gone.

Chapter Ten

Dawn hadn't even presented itself when she awoke to the ringing of the hotel phone. That would be her boss. Who else would be calling at such an hour? She put the pillow over her head and wished her life in New York would just go away. The phone persisted.

She hadn't expected to sleep, but in her heart she felt Kaikoa had done the right thing—to leave her alone. She was too emotional and really needed to sleep. *Thank God I slept.* Naked, on this sumptuous mattress, she wasn't ready to leave the warm womb of sleep. *Wait. Maybe it wasn't Dana calling* She scrambled for the phone.

"Wake up, sleeping beauty. There's a shell I want to show you. Meet me on the sand."

"When?"

"Now."

"Um, now's not the best time."

128

"Now is always the best time. See you—"

"Wait," She interrupted. "You took all my clothes. Even my pareo. I should be furious."

"I know. Let's skip that part."

April couldn't help but laugh and when she looked, she couldn't find the place where the anger had been.

After a long silence, he said, "The beach is empty. Wrap yourself in a sheet and come down here. Please."

"At least you said 'please.' You do realize any girl in her right mind would be angry to have her clothes taken."

"I'm sorry."

The magic words. He said them so simply. She couldn't remember the last time a man had genuinely apologized for his behavior.

He listened to her silence on the other end while she digested his words.

"The thought of you going down to the bar, in that dress with those red lips. If I couldn't have you, I was going to make sure no one else did."

His protectiveness wrapped its way around her heart. It was more than being wanted. She had never known a man who could so melt her anger. "I haven't even taken a shower or brushed my teeth. I'm surprised you left me my toothbrush."

"There's a shower on the beach. Bring one of those pretty hotel bars. I'll soap you all over."

She couldn't think of an answer. His words had created too strong an image in her mind.

"I have something for you," he said, painting a canyon full of mystery.

"What is it?"

"It's you."

April took the lead and said, "You come up. Five minutes. I'm jumping in the shower. I'll leave the door open." And she hung up. Everything inside her was smiling.

*   *   *

Moments later she stepped out of the shower and wrapped herself in a luxurious, soft towel. She looked up and he was standing there, watching her.

"Good morning, " she said.

He was wearing just his board shorts, and his chest was bare. Every toned muscle in his chest and abdomen was expanding and contracting.

"I ran up the stairs."

His hair was wet, probably from an ocean swim, and he seemed to be holding something behind his back.

"Where's my present? Or is it you?" April surprised herself at her new boldness.

"Here." He revealed her rolled up pareo, but when she reached for it, he playfully tossed it on the bed.

"You are a master of the tease," she said, as she brushed past him to the bed and flicked her wet hair across his bare shoulder.

"You're naked in a towel, and calling me a tease?"

She was happy to see her turquoise pareo.

"Go ahead. Unwrap." He walked to the bed and lay down on the rumpled sheet. *Did he mean unwrap herself or her present?*

She unfolded the fabric. Inside was a roll of parchment paper. She unrolled it and found an enchanting image of herself —a drawing of the moment from the night before, when she was undressing for him. He had captured the second of abandonment when she had tossed her dress.

Looking at this image brought back all the sensations of standing before him the night before. It was better than a photo, because it was re-imagined with his artist's hand. No one had ever looked at her with such reverence, much less immortalized the moment in an artful drawing.

"It's extraordinary."

"That is version six."

"Where are the other five?"

"I burned them."

"Why?"

"Oh, things weren't perfect. You know, perspective or the getting this part right," he drew the curve of her hip line in the air. "When it doesn't capture the spirit, I get infuriated and I have to destroy it."

"All part of the process of creation and destruction," she said.

"Exactly. I'm glad you understand artists."

"They've trained me well."

"Put on your pareo. I want to show you an extraordinary shell."

"Why didn't you bring it up?"

"You have to see it in its natural light. And with the waves washing over it."

"Where are my clothes?"

"At the front desk. You don't need them till you leave."

"And why is it that I don't need my clothes?"

"Just put on the pareo. In Hawaii that's dressed plenty." She hesitated.

"Come on, the sun's coming up." He tugged on her

towel. She snatched the pareo to cover herself just as her towel began to slide away.

* * *

He held the door of the elevator open. She hoped nobody would see her, with only a single piece of material tied around her. The day before she had seen other women, surfers, who had just removed wet bathing suits, barely clad in just their pareos, but they were used to being so close to Nature. He pushed the button for the lobby and when the doors closed, he stood behind her, drawing her close against him. With just a thin layer of silky fabric between them, she could feel the heat of his body blend with hers.

They rode in silence.

Except for the sound of her heart and the echo of his.

They arrived way too soon, but when they did he didn't move. Just reached over and pressed the button to go back to the top floor.

"I thought you were in a hurry to show me the shell," she giggled.

"I was. Once again I am reminded it never pays to rush."

She was flooded with anticipation of his next move. Slowly he slipped a hand inside the opening of her pareo. His touch was determined, but so exquisitely light it made her shiver.

Then—the elevator door opened. An older couple and a bellman, with a cart stuffed with luggage, stared at them.

"Going down?" the bellman said, his smile dripping with irony.

"No," Kaikoa said, and pushed the button to make the elevator door close. It took an eternity to do so. Kaikoa pushed it again as the old couple stared at April. She smiled apologetically in return, and moved a few inches away from Kaikoa. It was only a few inches, but it was enough to break the spell. Mercifully the doors finally crept shut but before they did, the old lady said to her husband, "Those two should get a room."

Needing support, April moved to the side wall of the elevator and leaned against it.

"Good idea," he said. "After we get the shell."

He moved to the opposite side of the elevator and studied her face to survey the damage to the soft mood of a moment before.

"Did you see the way that couple looked at me? How embarrassing."

"Yes. But before it was embarrassing, wasn't it a bit thrilling?"

April's smile admitted it was. But she wasn't ready to be approached and he must have sensed that, because he stayed on his side of the elevator.

"And the way the bellman smirked. Did he know you? Is this the kind of thing you do with all the girls?"

"No. But get it all out." Kaikoa waved his hands, like he was coaxing it out of her.

"Alright. Why does everybody call me Leilani?" April felt a tumble of frustrations from unasked questions pushing to get out. "And who is Leilani, your ex-wife?"

She saw a shadow cross his eyes.

"Leilani was my high school sweetheart."

She could see this was a sensitive subject. He looked

away and drifted back into a faded time. She resisted the temptation to go tearing into his memory like shoppers at a bargain basement sale. She would have to wait until he was ready to say more.

"She was sixteen," he said. "Surfing at Pipeline. Practicing for a competition the next day."

"She drowned?"

He nodded.

The elevator opened at the top floor but the magic of riding together was gone. Kaikoa reached over and pressed the lobby button again.

"I'm sorry," April said, not knowing what other words to add to fit such a loss of life and love.

They rode the rest of the way in silence.

* * *

It was just after dawn and the pink sky radiated a new day of possibilities. His eyes scanned the water line. She looked where he was looking, but just saw wet sand and pieces of broken shells. He led her to a spot on the beach where the waves were lapping the sand and he bent down and pointed to a perfect shell. She knelt beside an exquisite white shell less than a half-inch long.

"It's called a lined bubble or 'Bullina Lineata Gray.' It's very rare. The last time one was seen on this beach was after it washed up from a storm on Valentine's Day in 2001." He picked up the tiny shell and held it reverently in the palm of his hand. "Most people would walk right by it," he said. "But it's worth a lot of money. This is only the second one I've seen in my life." He lifted it closer for her to see. "This one's traveled a long way and survived a big storm."

"How do you know that?"

"See these stripes, and this wavy pattern?   Memorize this."

She tried her best to commit the pattern to memory, but it was so small. "You're the artist. You can probably paint it better than I can remember it."

"It's good to imprint the image on your brain."

"Why?"

"In case we see this shell again. I want you to be sure it's the same one."

"It's so fragile. Can we take it with us?"

"In Hawaii, we believe that everything has Mana, or spirit. We don't go around moving things without asking them for permission. Moving a rock or a shell that doesn't want to be moved. Well, that could be really dangerous for a person."

"I don't suppose your average tourist realizes that."

"No. People go around picking up all kinds of things, like lava rocks, as souvenirs, and take them back to the mainland. Then they get home, everything goes haywire and they have all kinds of bad luck."

"That can't be true."

"Legend has it that Pele, goddess of fire and volcanoes, is so angered when the rocks, which she sees as her children, are taken from her, that she exacts a terrible revenge on the thief. She is especially protective of volcanic rock and sand, two items tourists almost unthinkingly pocket as mementos of their vacations. After all, who would miss a shell or a rock? The post office has tons of rocks that people send back."

"What happens to the rocks?"

"There was one Tutu who would get the rocks, wrap

them in Ti leaves and pray for them. She would listen for days sometimes to make sure she was hearing correctly where they wanted to be returned. She had her kids helping her make the returns, because her legs weren't so good. But some of the rocks were too disturbed to talk. She returned about four hundred rocks before she died."

Kaikoa put the tiny shell in her hand.

"After that story, I'm almost afraid to hold it."

"Don't worry. I wouldn't have picked it up without asking for permission first."

"What are you going to do with it?"

"We get to spend a little time with it. Share our Mana with hers."

"What is Mana?"

"It is the spirit, or energy. All living things have Mana. Then we will bury it right where we found her."

April carefully put it back in his hands.

Her nervousness made him smile. "Don't be afraid. We're just going to talk with her."

"Okay. But I don't speak Shell."

"You can ask a question."

"Out loud or inside my head?"

"It's all the same to her."

April closed her eyes and the question was already there. She didn't speak it out loud, and after a moment she opened her eyes. He was watching her with the same patience she saw him give his young nieces and nephews.

"So, did I get an answer?"

"Yes."

"Well, what is it?"

"I don't know. It wasn't my question. I didn't think it

was my place to listen to the answer."

"Are you teasing me?" April suddenly felt annoyed. She punched his arm playfully, but it rattled the shell in his hand.

"Careful, *Wahine*. No, I'm serious. Just because you didn't hear the answer now doesn't mean it wasn't given. It just means you aren't ready to hear it yet. Like the answer is on hold in the Universe. You will hear it. Or see it. Or feel it soon."

"When? I asked a really important question. I need to know now."

"That's probably why you can't hear it now. You need to be relaxed to hear a shell speak."

April sighed, exasperated. "I can't believe I'm getting frustrated because I can't hear a shell talk."

"I'm sure it won't be long before you are willing to listen." He turned his full attention to the shell in his hand. "Okay. Our time together is passing."

Her heart skipped a beat. *Was he talking about the two of them?* But he located the spot in the sand.

Together they carefully buried the shell where they had found it.

"I think somebody needs breakfast in bed," Kaikoa said.

She dug her toes into the wet sand, feeling vaguely like she had just failed an important test.

"Come on." He led her back to the hotel.

As they stepped into the elevator she said, "I'm a city girl. You can't expect me to just be able to talk to shells just like that." This time they were not alone. A jumbo-sized vacationing couple stepped inside with them.

"You did just fine with the talking part. You just have to work on the listening."

"Did you two just get married?" the man asked Kaikoa.

"No, we just went to the beach to talk to a shell," Kaikoa responded.

The couple eyed April in her scant pareo, and Kaikoa wearing just his surfer shorts.

"Water's going to be calm today," Kaikoa offered the couple pleasantly.

They nodded politely, as if this wasn't exactly news. Then they rode the rest of the way in silence, and April was relieved when the elevator opened on the ninth floor. Kaikoa held the door open while April stepped out.

"Have a profound day," Kaikoa said to the couple as he left.

As the doors were closing, the man turned to his wife and said loudly, "Betcha those two just had sex on the beach."

Kaikoa and April laughed.

"Come on, I'll race you," he said.

And they tore off toward Room 936.

Chapter Eleven

April watched Kaikoa standing on the lanai. He was watching the waves lapping around the place where they had buried their shell.

She didn't want to interrupt him, but when he turned she offered the room service menu she was holding. "What do you want for breakfast?"

"You." He ignored the menu and pulled her close.

"I thought you said—" but she let him pull her toward him.

"Ignore what I said." His hand wandered down her neck to the knot on her brightly colored pareo—the only thing that covered her. His fingers explored the tied material, and even though April's body shivered at his touch, she pulled away. "Down boy. Didn't the *Honu* tell you to wait?"

"I don't care."

"So, we're switching roles again? Like we did when we ate the raspberry?"

"Yes," he said. "I'm tired of resisting. It's your turn. You're in charge of saying no."

April drew in her breath and forced herself to back away. She secured the tie that his fingers had loosened. She had a moment of compassion for how much self-control he had shown in their time together. Some small part of her knew his sense of timing was wise. Wiser than her wild impulse to grab him and ravish him. "I am going to step far away from you for sixty seconds," April declared. "When I come back, I want *you* to be clear about what you want, and stop giving me mixed messages."

He took a deep breath.

"Sixty whole seconds? Are you going to count?"

"Yes," she said.

"This is going to be a long minute."

"The longest, smartest minute of my life."

April walked back into the room, grabbed her card key and walked out the door. She stood in the hallway and leaned against the door with her eyes closed. She really wanted to listen deeply and get clear what the right move was, as she knew this was not just a casual encounter she could easily walk away from. But all she could hear was her heart pounding in her ears.

She started counting in her mind. She got to ten. Her mind replayed his words. "I am certain I could convince you that way. But I want your heart to decide." She remembered that kiss under the full moon and how it ignited something ancient. She had lost her place in counting in her head and switched to saying the numbers out loud.

He's willing to forego his principles if this is what I want.

140

The choice was all hers. All she had to do was say *yes* with all her heart and they would make love.

"Fifty-seven, fifty-eight, fifty-nine." She was counting so fast, she decided to start over. She needed to calm her own fires. As much as she wanted this, she didn't want their desire to overpower a wise choice.

If we make love, how will I ever return to my career, my life in New York? I have to be certain this is what I want.

That line in the sand said it all—that she was at a choice point, which was coming too soon. What about the years clawing her way up the ranks and gaining the respect of a difficult boss? Her five-year career plan was about to come to fruition.

This is not the time to lose my head and race into a new life.

She wondered if deep down he would respect her less for making the decisive move. That sounded so old-fashioned. In some ways he was a lover outside of time. At one moment he would show old-time chivalry, the next he seemed the most enlightened modern man she had ever met.

She knew she could take control. Change both of their destinies. But she wanted to pay close attention to timing. This was too important to rush. This is what he was teaching her. She had profound respect for his desire to honor their perfect timing. Knowing Kaikoa, he probably understood that the more patient he was, the more her desire to rush into his arms grew.

Making love will help me decide.

She had been outside the door for several minutes. And she congratulated herself for taking the time to really listen for the deeper wisdom.

Her hand shook as she slipped the key card back in the

slot.

She entered the room. His bare back was to her. He was still on the lanai, watching the waves. Her heart beat faster. She wondered what these moments of self searching had retrieved for him. She stood next to him on the balcony. He was silent. Such restraint.

She was suddenly flooded with an awareness that she had to look beyond her own needs and desires. How would it affect him to make love, and then have to put her on an airplane?

Finally he pointed toward the spot where they had just been on the beach. "Can you see that shimmer of energy around that spot? That's the *Mana* rising from all the love we put into our shell."

April did her best to let her eyes follow. To help her see, he took her arm and gently pointed it toward the spot on the beach below. The sensation of his body so close against her took over all of her senses. She was a white canvas suddenly ignited with his bright colors. No wonder his art awakened that sublime sense of aliveness. She closed her eyes. She wanted to live in his world where you could see the energy emanating from things that had been loved. She was in the center of a giant vibrating hum.

He let her arm float back down, and circled his around her, pulling her close. They gently swayed in sync with the sweet breeze. They moved when the wind blew, following the direction of its current. A dance with the wind.

She melted to his lead and it seemed they were one body. This was even more magical than the moment they had shared in the elevator. It was as if their connection in the elevator had prepared her to submit even more deeply now to his touch. Every moment they had spent together prepared her to receive him now.

"It's good to let the desire build," his breath whispered on her neck. It turned her into a rag doll in his arms. Her weight fell into his. She could feel his desire.

If only he would scoop me up in his arms and carry me to the bed.

April had never been with anyone so willing to savor desire without rushing to release the sensation. He had a certain mastery over time. Submitting to his control was thrilling.

She took his arm and raised the inside of his wrist to her lips, sweetly caressing and at the same time testing the boundaries of his self control.

"Salty," she said, enjoying his taste.

He made a low moan, enjoying her tease.

"I've got ocean salt all over me," he said. "I'm going to take a shower." And he unwrapped himself from her.

"Then what?" she said. She no longer wanted to feed the mystery.

"Then," he said without a hint of hesitation, "I will do whatever you want."

He walked toward the shower. But as he left her side, she felt a cold pull of energy. The hair on her arms raised. Something wasn't right.

"Wait," she said with an intensity that surprised her.

He stopped. He seemed to be watching something behind her. She was afraid to turn and look.

"I think . . . " Her voice wavered.

He waited.

"I think I will order us some breakfast."

"Good," he said, quietly.

She could see him swallow hard and something cross his eyes. She watched his chest rise and fall. Everything between them seemed to move into slow motion. The vein in his neck pulsed in time to her own racing heart.

"What do you want to eat?" Her words seemed bizarre. *He must think I'm nuts.*

"It makes perfect sense," he answered as if he had heard her.

He nodded. She nodded in return. Slowly he stepped inside the bathroom. The sense of a chill slowly dissipated. She was afraid to look behind her. Her hand shook as she dialed room service.

The minute she hung up, she couldn't remember what she had ordered. She took a few deep breaths to calm herself. She was still shaking slightly, not so much scared, as it felt that her molecules were moving faster, like she had entered a higher-energy force field.

Was that her? Was it Leilani? Is she slowing us down? Or keeping us apart?

She remembered something Tutu had said that night in the Bone Yard kitchen. She hadn't understood it at the time. Something about there still being someone in Kaikoa's bed.

How can I compete with his first love? How can I compete with a dead woman?

She knew she needed to speak to Kaikoa about this. Now. She looked over and saw that he hadn't completely closed the bathroom door.

Should I go in? Will we be alone in there? Will we be alone anywhere?

She listened to the sound of the shower and imagined him under the spray. To distract herself, she thought about her shower in Manhattan. It was so small she had barely enough room to change her mind. No, this shower made you feel like a queen—and even more so now with the presence of a king. She hoped the shower wouldn't wash away his natural male scent, something she was becoming addicted to.

How long had he been in there?

It seems like forever when every cell in your body is waiting.

After another eon, the water stopped. Her heart raced.

He emerged moments later, with just a towel around his waist, his dark hair dripping. She avoided looking at his tan, chiseled body.

"Was that her? Leilani?"

He nodded.

"Is she always with us?"

He shook his head no. "This was only the third time. Usually it's more."

"Is she always going to be with us?"

"I don't know."

April sat down in the padded rattan arm chair.

"You see why I can't just rush into something?" he said quietly. "It wouldn't be fair to you."

"How does she feel about us being together?"

He smiled shyly. It was the first time she had seen this vulnerability. "It's been her hand. Guiding some of the signs."

April met his smile. "Are you sure?"

He nodded. "It's just—there's a lot of timing involved. I don't understand it all myself."

April reached over and picked up the orchid from the dish. She playfully threw it at him. He caught it, and tossed it back.

145

There was a loud clatter in the hallway outside the door. He seemed rattled by it.

"You okay?" she asked.

"I didn't sleep much last night."

"What kept you up?" she teased.

"Images of you."

"Come, lie down until the food comes."

"Thank you," he nodded. "For understanding."

She took him by the hand and led him to the bed. It occurred to her that she wasn't the only one having a wild ride these past couple of days.

They lay down next to each other. He touched her hand lightly. "Just a short visit with the turtles," he said. "Then I'll be back with you."

He pulled her close to him and rested her head on his shoulder. Then he shut his eyes and dropped deeply into a gentle zone. His breathing was soft and warm against her cheek.

She watched the rise and fall of his chest. She had a wicked thought to slip her hand inside the towel, as he had done to her pareo in the elevator, but she was not quite so bold.

There was a knock on the door. It didn't wake him.

A female voice said, "Room service."

April was hungry, but she didn't want to move from this nectar of comfort.

The maid knocked louder.

"Yes?" April managed, and slid carefully out of his arms. Letting him sleep felt tender.

She opened the door and the maid entered, pushing a cart overflowing with breakfast treats. The maid looked over at Kaikoa asleep in just his towel, and averted her eyes.

"You must be hungry," the maid said.

"I think I over-ordered."

"Are you enjoying your vacation?" she said, as she waited for April to sign.

"Very much," April said, anxious for her to leave.

As the maid left, April saw her hide a smile.

When the door closed, it woke Kaikoa. April approached him and he looked at her with sleepy eyes.

"Get in" he said, pulling her towards him. "I want to serve you breakfast in bed."

"It's about time you served me," she said playfully.

"I know how you like it," he said. He had meant the cup of coffee which he poured for her. "Extra cream and half a brown sugar."

"You remembered." April made it sound like she thought this was silly, but she loved that he did.

"Look at all this food. Are we expecting a Boy Scout Troop?"

"I don't even remember ordering any of this."

He put the tray between them on the sheets, and opened a small jar of mango jam for her.

"Thanks. Do you want to know what I asked the seashell this morning?" she said.

"Was it about me?"

She stopped mid-bite on her croissant. Her eyes widened and she took the pastry out of her mouth. "If you're a mind reader—just tell me."

"I'm not. Why would I want to read minds when I can read shells? Shells are much clearer than minds."

"What do you mean when you say 'read a shell'?"

"There are signs everywhere. In the water, in the

clouds, in the rain. Once you realize they are communicating, you can't help but read them. When you find a Bullina Lineata before dawn it means you are at a crossroad. Nature communicates so directly."

"So what did I ask?"

"Something about you and me. Being together."

"I think you *are* reading my mind."

"Are you crazy? If I read your mind I'd be a mess. You've changed your mind about me five times in the three days that I've known you."

"I've changed my mind five times this morning—about whether or not to—ravish you.

"I know," he smiled. "You can't even decide whether to walk through an open bathroom door."

She stared at him with incredulity. How could he know this stuff?

"Okay, Mr. Shell Reader. What did the shell say about us?"

"I don't know. It's your shell."

"My shell? You found it."

"Yes, but I found it after spending the night remembering your image and drawing you."

"You stayed up all night—drawing me?

"Half the night. Since it was a full moon, I went for a swim." Kaikoa pointed towards the lanai.

"You were swimming—here?"

"Like Romeo outside your bedroom window, wondering how early I could go to the lobby and call you."

April almost spilled her coffee.

"You were outside my window? All night?"

"Most of it.

"You should have come up."

"If I did, then I wouldn't have found your shell." He turned back to his Eggs Benedict.

April couldn't get the image out of her mind of him swimming outside her window half the night.

How could I have slept through his proximity?

"You must be tired," she said. The words sounded so ridiculously obvious, but he nodded.

"Probably am."

"You need a nap?"

"I need—"

Their eyes met and they both smiled.

She wished he would say it out loud. *What would he do if I just let my pareo fall open?*

He ate hungrily. She wanted to test her powers of femininity. Could she overcome his reluctance? Or would he think less of her for trying?

"Your thoughts are very noisy this morning, Miss."

"Is that what the shell is telling you?"

"I don't need a shell to hear everything."

"So what am I thinking?"

"I have no idea."

Somehow she couldn't believe this was true. "What were *you* just thinking?"

"That these Eggs Benedict are fantastic."

Was he deliberately playing hard to get?

April rearranged her body into a more enticing position, but his focus was on breakfast. She grabbed the croissant and took a bite, but it felt dry and empty in her mouth. "I know on our first day you said you wouldn't move to New York. Any chance you—"

"No. I'm an Island Boy. I'm in the ocean almost every day. It's where I get my inspiration to paint. If I don't paint, my family doesn't eat. And you can see how many mouths I feed."

"I'm feeling really confused here. Sometimes I feel like you are seeing us together and then . . ."

"I am not confused about that."

"You're not?"

"Aren't we together right now?"

"I mean, walk off into the sunset. That kind of together. Past *now*."

"Don't get mad at me, but I think it is you who is not sure."

April wasn't mad. He was right. She wasn't sure.

"I just met you two days ago. It's not like I can just ask a flower, or a turtle or a shell—or a ghost."

"I understand. That must be very confusing to not be able to hear."

He gave her a look of genuine compassion, but with her nerves on edge, it just made her cranky.

"It's not like I can just suddenly start hearing the things you hear."

"We'll get your ears open. It takes practice."

He finished his Eggs Benedict and put the plate on the table. His calm about all of this was annoying to her, and she fought the desire to pick a fight—just to get a rise out of him. "So, bottom line is—if we are going to be together, I have to give up my life and my career and come and live with you in the Bone Yard?"

The drama queen won. She threw down her croissant and it splattered, leaving flaky crumbs between them. He stared at the flakes as if they were tea leaves with a message.

"I know you're annoyed with me right now," he said. "I know you want me to cast aside all your fears and ravish you. If I was certain that's what you really wanted, we wouldn't be talking. I would be making love to you this very moment. But I know you're not sure. That's why I haven't ripped that pareo off you."

April stared right back at him.

"Is that the only reason you haven't ravished me? Because you think I'm not sure? It's not because of Leilani?"

"It's because I know you're not sure."

"How do you know?" she demanded. "And don't tell me the turtles told you."

"For one thing, because *you* haven't ravished me. I left the door open in the shower, I lay next to you in only a towel, and I have kissed *you* under the moonlight. How many invitations can one gentleman give?"

April's frustration collapsed like a house of cards. She smiled with him. His kindness, like a wave's undertow, pulled back all her wild emotions.

She took a deep breath. The lines in her forehead softened and she settled back against the pillows.

How does he do this to me? He smoothes my mind like wet sand.

The space inside her where the anger was, almost ached —because of the familiar emotions leaving so totally. It was a little scary that he could shift her mood so quickly.

"Maybe we should make love," she said, without being able to meet his eyes. "Maybe it would help me choose."

He took the breakfast tray and moved it to the side and drew her in close. "I can't do that. Not until you are sure." He circled his strong arms around her. "And not just because of

151

you. I've never had a one-night stand. I can't make love to a woman unless I know we are going to be together for a long time."

"Is that true? That you've never had a one-night stand?"

"Yes."

It seemed like such a tender admission. "How many woman have you been with?"

He counted on his fingers. He stalled a moment. "Not including you?"

"I don't think I qualify as one of your conquests."

"You would be my fourth."

April swiveled to look him in the eye.

"Really? But all those women on the beach, in the restaurant, everywhere we go, they drool over you. I was sure they were all ex's."

"Some women love the challenge of the unattainable. You should hear what they say behind my back. Didn't my sister tell you they call me the *Ghost Lover*?"

"I thought that was because you live in the Bone Yard." Panic swelled in her heart, but she forced herself to ask the question. "Is there room in your bed for another woman? Because I don't know if I can handle this."

"I know."

"You know what?"

"That's why I said we have to take our time. So you can see if you can handle it."

"What exactly is it I have to handle here?"

"Me. My world. All the layers of my reality."

His vulnerability made her calm down. She was moved by his bravery in letting her so far inside his world.

"Is she going to be watching us when we make love?"

152

"No. She isn't like that."

"What is she like? How often is she here? I'm sorry, but I have to understand what I am getting into here. Or not getting into."

"Sometimes I don't see her for a year or two. Then I see her twice in two days. When I was younger and about to make a foolish choice she would show up and make some mischief. But I wised up pretty quickly after a few visits."

"Why does that lady in the bikini store, and your family, call me Leilani?"

"Because in those moments she walked in behind you. They can see her."

April sat up. Goose bumps prickled on her arms and the hair stood up again. "Isn't

"You call this chicken skin, don't you?"

"Yes."

"Is that her? Is she here now?"

"No. She'll never come if it frightens you. That was someone else."

"How many ghosts do you have?" She got up and went toward the bathroom.

"That was just someone passing through," he offered.

"This is just all too weird."

"You need time. I'll go downstairs and get your suitcase." He deftly slipped his board shorts on under the towel. Surfers were experts at dressing and undressing without privacy.

April didn't object. But before he closed the door he turned to her.

"You okay?"

"Yeah, I'm okay," April said. "I just seriously need a lot

of time to think."

He seemed encouraged. "If you're going to live in the Bone Yard, you're going to have to get used to having more than one layer of reality."

"I think it's a little soon to talk about me living in the Bone Yard."

"That's why I said '*if.*'"

He opened the door and left. She followed him out and called to him as he approached the elevator. "Are you that sure about me?"

He sighed.

"Is that a 'no'?"

"That's a 'don't be mad at me, but the turtles told me not to answer that question for you.' They said you had to come to clarity on your own."

The elevator door opened and he stepped inside.

She stood in the doorway of her room watching the space where he had been standing. Was it her imagination, or was there a shimmer in his place?

Chapter Twelve

After several moments April went back inside her room. She laid down on the bed, her pulse throbbing.

Was he coming back? When?

He had a wicked habit of disappearing without any information about his return. And it wasn't as if she could text him on his non-existent cell phone. She ran through a speech in her mind about why he "must have a cell phone if they were going to be together." But she knew it would fall on deaf ears.

She drifted into a near-sleep place. She had the sensation that he was still next to her on the bed. It was so strong that she actually reached out to touch the space where he had been moments ago. It thrilled her and frightened her at the same time.

Just then a gust of wind blew the curtains on the open sliding glass door of the lanai. The orchid lifted in the breeze and fell to the floor. Her heart beat faster. She went to pick it up. She inhaled it, but it had no fragrance she could detect. She had an impulse to take it to the lanai and toss it over.

It made no sense, but she followed the inner "instruction." She stepped onto the lanai and looking out at the ocean, she tossed the flower over the balcony.

At that exact moment she saw Kaikoa running out onto the sand below her balcony. He raced, and caught the flower just before it touched the sand.

He touched it to his heart and looked up at her, nine floors up.

He put his hands to his mouth, and was yelling something, she couldn't hear the words. Others on the beach looked up at her and gave the shaka sign in support.

"Come back up," she yelled in her loudest voice. But he couldn't hear her words either. She waved wildly, motioning for him to return. He didn't hesitate. He ran inside.

* * *

The moment that he knocked on the door of room 936 she swung the door open. He was beaming.

"I'm so proud of you," he exclaimed. "You heard the flower."

People passing in the hallway tried to pretend they weren't listening. She motioned for him to step inside.

"Well, I can't say I 'heard it'—like in words—like we're using now. I just felt something. Like an impulse."

He nodded. "That's how it starts."

He sat down and took a drink of the cold coffee in his cup.

"I really want to understand this." she said. When you

say you talk to the turtles, or the shell, or the flowers—do you mean in language?"

"Are you really in the mood to listen?"

"Yes. I obviously need some educating here."

"Alright." He held the orchid in his hand that she had tossed over the balcony, and presented it to her.

"First you harmonize with the energy of the flower." She accepted the flower he held reverently in his hands. "You want to tune into its specific energy."

He sat down on the floor, cross-legged, and she sat across from him. She watched as Kaikoa put all his concentration on the flower.

He cupped his hands around the flower, as if receiving an energy transmission from it into his hands. She could see a slight waver, as if his hands were detecting subtle emanations.

"What is it that you are doing?"

"I am tuning myself to *its* specific frequency. Here, your turn."

He presented the flower in his hands so she could 'feel' the energy.

"How do I…"

"Just let yourself be *touched* by the flower."

April cupped her hands a few inches above the flower and tried to tune in, to sense whatever energy the flower might be sending.

"I think I feel something. But I might just be making it up."

"Tell me what you feel, and I'll tell if it is the same thing I felt."

"It feels—this is going to sound weird—bruised."

"Excellent."

She beamed, even if she didn't quite believe any of this.

"But that was the other flower. The one you tore up."

April sank. She looked over at the torn flower, feeling a new wave of remorse.

"Don't be down. You heard perfectly. You just tuned into the *other flower's* frequency."

"So, every flower has its own specific frequency?"

"Well, that's a more advanced truth, like a hummingbird can sense the difference between each unique flower."

"I'm just a human. I can't be expected to be as smart as a hummingbird."

"Agreed."

"You could at least argue."

"Just start with the basics. For now, just think of it as if you were connecting with the entire flower kingdom. It's a realm of living energy."

April tried harder. Her brow furrowed.

He laughed.

Outside in the corridor a room service waiter rolled a cart noisily down the hall. It shattered the potent peace inside the room. She tried to get her focus back on the flower.

"You're trying too hard," he said. "Just relax. Let the flower come to you."

She relaxed and actually felt a gentle wave of sweetness.

"Yes. That's it."

"Are you sure I'm not just imagining?"

"I can tell it's real because when you are calm, it's like a tone or hum, I can hear it."

"You can *hear* my emotions?"

"Sometimes. If I am paying attention. Sometimes they are very loud."

"Sorry."

"It's okay. You're just learning about energy."

April put the flower down on the bed next to them. She got up and paced, feeling she needed to shake off the powerful sensations.

"I'm not sure if I like this. It's kind of weird. That's like mind reading."

"People are *broadcasting* all the time. Every emotion has its own frequency. It's one of the ways dogs and cats know what's going on inside you. Remember the way my dogs greeted you?"

"I thought they were just friendly. Don't they greet everyone that way?"

Kaikoa laughed. "When they don't like someone, it's loud and clear."

"My cat is like that. Certain people, she's just not interested in getting to know them."

"Yes. You can't fool an animal. They read you perfectly."

"Glad I passed your dog's test." April gave an exaggerated sigh of relief. "But I am just not as smart as your average dog."

"You can learn. With practice you can learn how to lock onto the right signal. Then, the music comes through." He pointed toward the ocean. "The dolphins can hear your emotions."

"What's it like to *hear* emotions. Doesn't that drive you crazy?"

"It can. Sometimes it does. Walking through the lobby

here, I feel like twenty different radio stations are on at once. Do you see why I wouldn't do so well in New York City?"

April sat back down. Her mood was somber. It made perfect sense. But it wasn't a reality she was ready to face. They sat for awhile with their private thoughts.

Two grey striped doves arrived and perched on the balcony. They seemed to be watching them. April looked up and studied them.

"Do all animals hear? Even those birds? Are they listening to my emotions right now?"

Kaikoa looked over at the birds for a moment.

"They just came for your croissant."

She laughed. Kaikoa stepped over to the breakfast tray and broke off an uneaten piece and tossed some crumbs toward them. They leapt off the ledge and came down to feast.

"I sort of felt something. It felt nice. But I can't imagine asking a question and hearing an answer the way you do," she said.

"It takes practice. I've been doing it my whole life. My family does it. It's easier for me because it's in my culture. You have to cross a divide of not believing."

"Are you saying white chicks can't listen to flowers?"

"I'm saying you have to be patient. You have to practice. You have to open your mind to the possibility before you can have the experience."

The birds finished eating and looked up at Kaikoa. He made some perfectly accurate bird sounds and they sang back to him. This went back and forth for a few rounds. Then Kaikoa laughed.

"That one on the left is funny." He crumbled up another piece of croissant, which they gobbled up enthusiastically and then they flew off into the blue sky.

He sat back down on the floor, his back leaning against the bed. She slid in place next to him, feeling the warmth of his body, and the rise and fall of his breath.

"Okay, teach me. I want to be able to ask flowers questions."

"You have to leave the *energy of the question* behind. If you get so obsessed with the question, you won't be able to hear the answer."

"You mean the energy of the question can interfere with hearing?"

"Yes, because the energy signature or frequency of the question is a different tone from the answer tone."

"So, how do I hear the answer tone?"

"You have to listen for the flower's pulse," he said as if it was the easiest thing in the world. "You might not want to tear up any more flowers in their presence."

"Do all the flowers hate me now?"

"Flowers have better things to do than hate people." He took her hands and cupped them, then placed the flower in her hands.

"Don't just stare at it. Soften your eyes so you can *perceive* the essence with your heart. Calm your energy down to match or resonate with the flower."

April could feel herself calming down as she focused on the flower's essence.

"That's good," he said.

She didn't know how long they had been quiet. When her eyes met his, something was different. She wasn't sure what, but she felt soft inside. There was a tone in her ear she hadn't noticed before.

He nodded. "That's it. When you feel like you're in sync with the flower, quietly focus the question in your mind. Don't hold the question hard. Once you've focused it, then you let it float away, on a gentle breeze."

"Then the flower will answer you?"

"If you are listening and not yelling. Some questions have so much emotional charge they just sound to the flowers like yelling."

"Nobody likes being yelled at."

"Right. Then it's like crossed wires, and you're only hearing your own tangled thoughts. That creates a communication disconnect and you can't hear the answer."

This was energizing, but she needed a break. She put the flower down. Much as she wanted to succeed, it was still a little too far outside her usual boundaries of reality.

"And another thing about talking to flowers." He tenderly picked it up. "They don't always answer the moment you ask. They have their own sense of timing. That's why she made such a good teacher."

"She?"

"*That* orchid. From when we had breakfast the first morning." He pointed to the orchid that was still on the dresser. April had saved it.

"How do you know that was the same orchid, from our first breakfast?"

"Once you talk to a flower, it becomes as unique as a person."

"Could you please apologize for me? For the one I tore up and—"

"And threw at me," he said. "We can plant a tree to make that *pono*. Tutu can help us with that."

"What does *pono* mean?"

"To make it right."

"Could you at least tell the flower that I'm sorry I did that."

"Of course. I did that right away. Fortunately, flowers don't hold grudges or the whole planet would be destroyed."

"You never did tell me what the flower said. I mean the breakfast flower."

"She said that you've never said 'Yes' with all your heart. And that I should do nothing to rush you."

It was true. April had never really fully said 'Yes' to anyone or anything. Of course she had said partial yes's to people, places, and the minutiae of life. She had accepted dinner invitations, job offers and free magazine subscriptions from her credit cards. It hit her like a huge wave that this was so true. She had never said 'yes' with one hundred percent of her heart to the really big choices in life.

"When my husband proposed to me—my ex-husband," she added quickly, "I was so unsure what I wanted, he finally had to say 'yes' for me. And in the end I let his sureness override my own. I don't even know what it feels like to say 'yes' with all my heart. I think I've always been saving a part of myself in reserve."

"That's why it's so important this time that you find your own true 'yes,'" he said. "It hasn't been easy to not just reach over and tear that flimsy piece of fabric off you."

"Really?" She tried to get the sixteen-year-old sound out of her voice, but she couldn't help it. "You mean that?"

"I spent four hours swimming in the ocean under your window trying to resist the desire to . . ." He laid down on the bed and let the silence speak for itself.

April got up and paced back and forth in front of the bed. This was a lot to take in. At least she wasn't the only one having this burning desire. That sent a warm jolt of energy from her toes to her teeth. She looked at him, admiring his strength of character. *It must be love, to have this level of restraint.*

"Please don't test my resolve any more," he said. "I am a man, after all."

"Okay," she smiled. "I'll try not to."

"Don't try. Just stop."

"Stop how?"

"Stop being so sexy. Put some clothes on."

"I would if I had some. Somebody took them away."

"Right. I'll go get them." He sat up too quickly and held his head in his hands to steady himself.

"Down boy." She pushed him back on the bed. "They can wait. It's true, what the flower said. I think I've lived my whole life amazed that other people seem so sure about what they want—that I just end up joining their parade."

It was a vulnerable admission. He responded by pulling her closer to him. She laid down next to him.

"I had a cousin who was a ukulele teacher. He once said to me, "To say 'Yes' with all your heart to one single moment is to say yes to all existence.'"

As if in reply to the rich silence of this idea, two spotted doves landed on the lanai. Kaikoa listened to their cooing and chirped perfectly—the three of them involved in a conversation.

"You're talking to the doves now?"

Kaikoa nodded.

"Well, tell me. What are they saying?"

"It's hard to put into words. They don't talk in sentences.

"Try."

"It's more like feeling-pictures."

"So, you see the message?"

"See and feel. It's like I open my heart to them and listen. And then I get this understanding. You would probably call it an *emotional data download* where this picture pops into focus."

"Can you describe the feeling picture?"

"Not really. It's more like a knowing. The doves showed me this image, which was a pattern of swirling grey energy with these pink tones. I recognized it as your confusion."

"How did you know it meant *I* was confused?"

"Because I'm not. The pink was this awesome awakening, like daybreak." He used his hands to draw what he was seeing in the air. "But there was this other energy overlaying it. Competing for your attention. Like you are holding two competing realities at the same time."

"That's exactly how I feel."

"So, that's why we have to wait. Until you choose which reality is true."

April stared at him. He was making more sense than anyone ever had.

"I don't understand how in some moments you can read my mind, and then in other moments you haven't a clue."

"I told you, I don't read your mind. No offense, but it gets pretty gnarly in there." He pointed to her head. "I'd rather talk to your feet." He moved down to the bottom edge of the bed and took one foot in his hands. "May I?"

"I never turn down a foot massage."

He began soothing away the little knots of tension around her arch, which gave way to his firm fingers. She was glad she had taken the time to get a pedicure the first day. A pleasurable moan escaped her lips.

"Thank you," he said in response to her moan.

"Okay, I just need one thing explained. How can I be in this moment and not have thoughts about the future, or the past, or—"

"Is that what you're worried about? Of course you're going to have thoughts. We all have thoughts about the past or the future."

"Sometimes I wish I could just erase my mind," she said.

"It's like trying *not* to think about a purple elephant. As soon as you say the words 'purple elephant' that's all you see."

"Exactly," she said. "You can't *unthink* something that is part of your world."

"How does this feel?" he tried a sliding pressure touch.

"Too good for words."

"But that won't stop you from using them."

She laughed. He touched another spot that was tender and she jerked away. "Ow. But don't stop."

He continued the massage, not avoiding her tender spots. "The idea is not to exclude it, but to *include it all*. Allow the past, present and future to melt into the present moment."

"So, the present can include the past and the future?"

"Right. You've seen how my present includes my past. And future."

"Oh, that feels so good. Maybe that's the secret. Make now so good that it erases the future."

"Glad you like it. This whole thing about "now" is that it isn't fixed. It's always expanding and contracting, breathing, waving in and out. Sometimes it opens to include the past or the future, sometimes it contracts into a single cell of momentary awareness."

"I wish I knew what you were talking about."

"I'm just saying that in this mode, all timing is perfect. This is very different from seeing life moving in one direction on a linear timeline. In that mode you almost always feel late for something."

"I always feel late for something. Or that there is something more important that I should be doing."

He switched to her other foot. "You don't resist those pulls or jerks from the past or future, but you direct your focus to the present."

"So it's about choosing your focus."

In that moment two doves flew back and landed on the banister on the lanai.

"See, she understands," he said to the birds. He switched from the deeper touch to a softer pulsing and tapping.

"Oh, that is so good," she moaned. "Are those the same two birds who were here before?"

"They're not. But their friends told them we're nice."

"Because we share our breakfast."

"Yeah. That too."

April was certain she saw the birds bob their heads in response.

And with that the doves flew away. Their mission accomplished.

"Goodbye, doves," April said, surprised she could actually feel the communication between them was complete.

"You see? It's not so hard," he said.

"How do I know I'm not making this up?"

"In the beginning you won't know the difference between hearing a genuine message and just your imagination talking, but after a lot of practice, you will be able to hear and feel the distinction."

"Could you teach me to…" April couldn't get the words to come out. "Never mind."

"Could I teach you to *never mind*?" he teased.

"I mean, if I wanted to talk to my parents. I'm not saying I do. I'm saying if I ever really needed to, you know."

"Yes."

"*Yes*, as in you know, or *yes* as in you could teach me?"

"*Yes,* as in I know. And *Yes* as in I could teach you. When you're ready. To trust the experience."

"That's going to takes a lot of trust."

"True. Does your foot trust my hand?"

He tapped the bottom of her foot with his thumb.

She nodded.

"Say *yes* to this exact moment."

"Yes."

"That's it. The rest will take care of itself."

"You make it sound so easy."

"It is. That's how you love Hawaii Time."

"Yes" she said with all her heart.

Her whole body melted—not just into him—but into the entire experience of saying *yes*.

Chapter Thirteen

The foot massage had relaxed her so much that she drifted into sleep. When she awoke, she saw he had retrieved her clothes and suitcase. Either he moved with stealthy silence, or she must have really been out of it. There definitely is something about the sweet Hawaiian air that is very conducive for sleeping.

He stood on the lanai and watched a gecko crawl along the railing. She waited until it was gone, in case Kaikoa was talking to him, then she said, "Do you have any idea what you're asking of me?"

"Yes, I do."

She sighed, and laid her head back down on the pillow.

"I should go get the truck," he said after a long silence. "Take your time getting ready."

April nodded her thanks. It seemed too hard to put her thoughts into words, and she was glad to have this time alone

169

to gather her thoughts.

When she heard the door close, she got up and headed for one last luxurious shower. After the shower she debated about calling her boss, but she decided she would call from the airport. After all, it wasn't that she had any news her boss wanted to hear.

She stepped onto the lanai one last time to watch the waves. This was only her third day in Hawaii, and already she couldn't imagine not having this view of eternal motion in her life. There is something about the color blue that soothes the soul.

But my whole life is in New York. How do I walk away from everything I've worked so hard for?

As she dressed in her navy blue suit from the day she arrived, she tried to remind herself of all the great things about New York—the culture, the theater, independent movies, unlimited art galleries, exotic cuisines from every country in the world—delivered at all hours, sophisticated conversations about things that mattered. *Or did they? Talking to Kaikoa is richer than all that chatter.*

Suddenly her New York list felt more like a travel ad than a life. *Am I out of my mind for leaving? Or out of my mind if I stay? I wish I knew which.*

Kaikoa was right to leave her to herself at this moment. She was a wreck, and would have picked a fight about nothing, just to distract herself from her mental torment. She tore off her navy blue business suit. It felt heavy and artificial, even though it normally made her feel powerful and professional. She changed into her workout clothes, a jogging suit, but it felt too warm, and the wrong mood. Changing for the third time she wanted to wear the dress she had bought here. She struggled with getting out of her skirt, and everything seemed to be spinning around her.

All I have to do is tell him I will stay—and the spinning will stop. Or will a whole new spin just begin?

In New York City all she had was a sublet furnished apartment, but in Manhattan that was the Taj Mahal. And she had her dream job—minus the daily boot camp with a retired colonel for a boss. She did have the perfect cat. Her neighbor, Mrs. Markovitz, loved keeping Angelina, and would be only too happy to keep her a while longer. She had read warnings in *Cosmo* about vacation romances and she needed to be sure.

I could stay with Kaikoa for a month and see if it's real.

Just two words, "I'll stay" is all it would take. She could take the time on the ride to the airport to make the decision. And if I say those two words, he would smile and swing the car around and go—go where? She could hardly afford even one night in the hotel.

Do I really want to live in the Bone Yard?

Much as she loved his family, could she really live without electricity and wi-fi, and having the whole neighborhood over for dinner every night? To say nothing of visitors from the grave.

It was time to face reality. They lived in different worlds.

* * *

Kaikoa drove the truck to the airport slowly, easily, quietly. If his mind was churning, he didn't expend any words to reveal it. April's mind was a one-woman war zone. His silence made the noise in her head louder. He held her hand when he wasn't shifting gears, but she found herself getting agitated when his hand delayed in returning to hers. Questions rubbed like sandpaper in her brain and forced her to speak.

"Did you even read the contract?" was her first disturbed arrow, piercing the uneasy quiet.

"I read two pages. They put me to sleep."

April sighed and shifted her weight away from him. *Couldn't he tell she was irritated?* "So, you don't have electricity in the house except in the kitchen." She continued the verbal charge. "And you don't have internet connection."

"The neighbors do. The Nehoa family would let you use theirs."

"What about bathrooms? I didn't even see a shower."

"Six showers."

"Six? I didn't see any—"

"They're all in one room."

"Communal showers?" She didn't bother to disguise her horror.

"You can turn them so you get all six spraying at you. The kids love it."

"I'm sure they do."

"It's kinda wasteful so we only do the six-way for special occasions."

April had visions of summer camp. It wasn't her cup of tea.

As if he read her thoughts, he added, "How about if I build you your own dream bathroom?"

"You could do that?" April loved that idea. "I mean you know how to plumb—"

"I built the one we have now. You design it. I build it."

"Could it be upstairs? With a window? Looking out at

172

the trees? With a huge tub? With those spray jet things?"

"Yes. To everything," he said. "It'll be just for you. And anyone you might care to invite."

It had always been her secret dream to have the perfect bathroom with a huge tub and a view and the colors just the way she wanted. She let her mind wander, designing and decorating in her mind. She looked over at him. He had just the hint of a smile but it was enough to make the crazy part of her spin out.

"So you think you can buy my whole life with the perfect bathroom? That I will give up everything I have worked for—for a tub?"

"A *huge* tub," he corrected.

"You're talking like I'm coming back. I have no idea what I'm going to do. I have a whole career in New York. I've almost achieved my five year plan goals in four years."

"I'm not surprised."

"You do realize I haven't made my decision? It's very old fashioned to expect the woman to give up everything to come and live in a Bone Yard with some man."

"I'm not 'some man.'"

"What would I do in Hawaii? I doubt there are even any jobs for artist reps. I can't just be a housewife, sitting around making quilts and bread pudding."

He surprised her by pulling the car over onto the shoulder of the highway. Other cars whizzed past them.

"What are you doing?" she asked.

He leaned over to kiss her. Slowly. Deliberately. Softly.

It worked.

"You're trying to pick a fight with me," he said, his lips brushing against her ear. "But I know it's just you trying to get me to tell you what to do. And we both know you need to decide what you want, for yourself."

"Yeah." She settled down into a slow smile. "But at least act like you're upset, because I might *not come back*"

He looked into her eyes.

Does he already know what I will do? How could he? She didn't know herself. Yet he seemed to know more about her in three days than anyone ever had—including herself.

"I just wish you would be more upset that I'm leaving" she said, sounding and feeling like a six-year old.

"You're upset enough for both of us. First rule of saving a drowning man. Don't go and drown with him. Or *her,* as the case may be."

"Okay, but you are upset, right? I mean, have you considered seriously that I might not come back? Or it might take a year. I can't just pack up my whole world in an hour"

"Do you have a lot of stuff?"

"What?" The calmer he sounded, the more agitated she got.

"Do you have a lot of furniture and big possessions?"

"Actually, I don't. After I found out my husband was cheating on me with my best friend from high school, I couldn't live with all the stuff he and I had bought and shared together. I packed up my turtles and whatever I could fit into a taxi and left that night and went to a hotel. The next day I took a furnished sublet."

"Ouch." That would explain your shell talking about coming through a hurricane," he said, more to himself than to her.

"I thought the sublet was just till I got my feet on the ground and I was ready to get my own stuff. Guess I haven't

174

been ready. I've been living out of five suitcases, a laptop and an iPhone for four years."

"Good," he said. He watched for a break in the flow of traffic and pulled back onto the highway. "How many hours does it take to pack up five suitcases and an iPhone?"

"That's not the point," she yelled.

"Good. Scream some more. It will make the tears less salty."

And that was it. She didn't say another word and they drove the rest of the way in prickly silence until he pulled up at the airport terminal.

Chapter Fourteen

Back in New York it was as if someone had turned off the colors on the world. Even the trees with their skimpy leaves seemed dull and drab, covered in a layer of sooty lifelessness. Had New York always looked this way, or was it just because it was about to rain again?

Sitting at her desk at work she stared at the pile of colorful invitations to gallery openings that she was sifting through, deciding which ones to enter into her e-calendar. She glanced at the time at the bottom of her computer screen. She had been sitting there for over an hour, and had only entered one event to attend. Normally she could go through a packet twice this size in about fifteen minutes, and decide which events were worth the precious time it would take to attend, and which invites were destined for the re-cycle bin.

Bleary-eyed from crying the night before, she stared at one with sixties-style bright colors, designed like a hallucinogenic acid trip. She didn't know how long she had

176

been hypnotized by the image, when she heard Kristy's voice at the door.

"I wouldn't waste my time on that one. His work is very derivative," Kristy said, leaning on her doorway, as if she wanted an invite to come further inside.

"What?" April struggled to focus on what Kristy's words meant. "Yeah, sure. I was just trying to imagine a time when neon orange, lime green, and bright yellow seemed like an artistic statement."

"So, I heard you came back from Hawaii empty-handed." If Kristy was trying to hide the pleasure in her voice, she hadn't done a very good job.

"Guess you could say that." April went back to pretending to work. She re-entered the event she had already placed on her calendar, just to look busy, hoping Kristy would get the hint. She didn't.

"You want to sign the card for Leslie?" Kristy walked toward her, carrying a big happy greeting card with a pink stork on the cover.

April nodded. She looked at the card, reading some of the words others had already written while she tried to get her scrambled brain to remember who Leslie was. After reading a few inscriptions she remembered it was the pregnant young receptionist she saw every day. April read a few more inscriptions and copied the word "Congratulations." Then after a long moment added, "Love April."

Kristy stared at her as she handed the card back to her.

"You usually have more to say."

"I wanted to leave space for others," April said. Even as the words left her lips they sounded like an inane excuse.

"Remember, we're having her office shower today?

Greek food."

"Yeah, of course," April was working hard to sound normal, and wasn't sure at all it was working.

"Well, see you at the meeting later."

"Meeting?" April felt a cold chill run up her spine. Nothing was computing.

"Creative!"

"Of course. Creative meeting. In an hour.

Kristy looked at her watch. "In forty-three minutes."

"Right. I'm just a little jet lagged. With the time change."

"Sure," Kristy said, with her pasted on smile. "Have an espresso. Get your game face on."

"Go Team!" April answered dully with one of her boss's favorite slogans.

"Go Team!" Kristy replied with what appeared to be genuine enthusiasm.

Mercifully she left April's doorway. April wondered how she was going to appear even vaguely presentable, when she had never felt worse in her life. She got up and closed the door behind her. Sometimes having a door to close felt like a deep gasp of air when you have been underwater too long.

* * *

The Creative Meeting, which was their usual Monday morning routine at Consolidated Branding seemed endless— and worse—pointless. It was as if April had swallowed the hallucinogenic post card of the 60's artist's vision. Nothing felt real, and people seemed to be speaking in either slow motion or way too fast. April wished she had gotten more than two hours sleep. There was no way she could function like this. But she had pulled all nighters, and red-eye flights, before, and still functioned. This was not just tired. This was heartbreak. No way to sugar coat it. This was unbearable.

She looked out at the gray skyline. She could see people buzzing around in the building across the street. "What was so important?" she thought, and for a moment she wasn't sure if she had said those words out loud. April hadn't even realized she had been staring out the conference room window for a very long time, until she heard her boss's voice calling to her.

"April, are you part of this meeting?"

Everyone at the conference table was staring at her.

"Even though her body returned three weeks ago, April is still in Hawaii," Dana said. "Is there anything you would like to contribute to this brainstorming session, April?"

"Yes," April improvised. "I think this campaign is pedestrian and colorless. I don't see why any of us should be so satisfied with the ordinary."

The room was quiet enough to hear the judgments in her co-workers brains. It rattled her that she felt she could hear their thoughts. What extra-sensory part of her brain had Kaikoa turned on? And how could she get it to turn off? It was not comfortable and she wasn't even sure if she was making it up or if it was real.

This must be what he experiences when he can hear into the silence.

She had a pang of compassion for the way he felt unexpressed emotions. It could be burdensome to have such sensitivity. Eighteen eyeballs glared back at her. She wanted to say, *stop staring at me,* but she held the words back. After all, with her recent words she had just insulted the nine most creative brains in the company and there was no way to pretend she meant something nicer.

"Well, April," Dana bristled, "by tomorrow morning at 8 AM, I expect to see your colorful, extraordinary ideas for a new campaign."

April swallowed hard. She knew she was right about the campaign but she had no new ideas to replace it. She was pretty sure everyone in the room could tell from her silence she had nothing.

"We're done here," Dana said, reading the room.

Everyone got up and gathered their iPads. No one looked at April. She wondered what on earth could have possessed her to come up with such a comment—even though it was true—much less how she was going to think up anything any better.

* * *

Kaikoa's six-year-old niece, Hoku, hugged the doorway of his open-air art studio. He stood in front of a new, unfinished painting of Red Ginger. It was the kind of flower with bright green leaves you would see often on trails and it flourished in his backyard. The bright red interlaced bracts are unique and often form a perfect diamond shape, rising to an apex which is why people often gaze at them for meditation purposes.

Hoku could see his eyes were closed, the paint brush still in his hand and she knew not to interrupt her uncle when he was in his "inside place."

She skipped back to the kitchen.

Tutu looked up from the pot she was stirring. "He's not

coming in for dinner, is he?"

Hoku shook her head 'no.'

"No worries. Like one pig in emu hole in ground fire. Takes time to cook."

Hoku nodded, but then hurriedly said, "We're not going to eat Uncle?"

Tutu laughed. "No. But he is marinating something fierce."

* * *

April reached for the last tissue in the box next to her bed. It was the third box she had been through since she arrived home three weeks ago. At eleven PM her cell phone rang, startling her cat. The caller ID indicated it was her boss. She didn't want to answer it, but Dana would just leave text messages that she would have to read through, and e-mails that would ruin the taste of her morning coffee.

She blew her nose, tested her voice to make sure it didn't reveal she had been crying and answered the phone.

"How are those extraordinary ideas coming along?" Dana said flatly, without bothering to say hello.

"I think you know," April said. As awful as the truth made her sound, it was a relief to be using it more often.

"Have you heard from Kaikoa since you've been back?"

"No."

It was the first time her boss had mentioned him. She had been uncharacteristically mute when it came to asking about him. April knew this polite détente wouldn't last forever. Still, she wasn't prepared with an official explanation.

"You didn't go and do something ridiculous, like sleep with him, did you?"

"No."

"That's a relief. You think there's any chance if I sent you back you could convince him? I tried, but I couldn't talk The Freeman Group into anything other than Kaikoa's artwork."

"No." April didn't see the point of explaining anything when there wasn't anything good to say. Besides, she had been so exhausted with fighting with herself for the past three weeks she had no energy left to tangle with her boss.

"That's not what I wanted to hear. I wish I'd never shown them Kaikoa's designs because now it's all they want."

"You knew we didn't have a deal." April thought better about making her boss wrong, and said no more.

"The day before you left they were in my office and saw the designs on my desk."

"No one sees anything you don't want them to see."

"They just got extremely excited about them, and I thought—first time artist—I took a gamble we could get him to sign."

"Kaikoa doesn't do anything predictable," April said.

Both women were silent. Each probably musing over their own version of how annoying that is.

"April, you've been walking around like a zombie for three weeks. Are you trying to tell me you aren't interested in this job anymore?"

"I don't know."

Silence on the other end.

"That is not the answer I was expecting from my career-climbing protégé."

"I know."

"You need to get yourself into some serious knowing. You've worked your buns off for nine years to earn your position at Consolidated Branding. I want to see you in my office tomorrow morning at 7:15."

"Okay," April said, feeling like a dozen lizards were crawling up her back.

"Be prepared to show me that you are willing to fight to keep your job."

* * *

Kaikoa was painting in his open air studio behind the house. A cat meowed, and he looked up to see a beautiful orange tabby walking towards him.

"Who are you?" he said. "I've never seen you before." The cat came up and rubbed against his leg. He leaned down to pet her and she began to purr.

"Did you wander off? Are you hungry?" He reached over to his half-eaten *lau-lau* sandwich and put the plate down on the floor. The cat took a few nibbles but seemed more interested in him.

"Food is not your priority. Someone must be feeding you. Probably wondering where you are."

Meow.

"You're not from this neighborhood. There must be something you've come to tell me."

The cat leaped up on his lap as if Kaikoa was her old friend.

"I see. You want me to adopt you. I hope you like chickens and roosters and frogs and dogs."

Kaikoa continued to pet the cat. And she purred even louder.

"Yes, I do think you are very *puuurrrtty.* Well, I don't usually paint cats. Yes, I agree cat paintings are very popular."

The cat sat up and faced him with unblinking eyes.

"Oh, I see, you have some very cute ideas of your own." Kaikoa chuckled, as he petted the cat under her ears. "What? Wait. Too many ideas at once. You're starting to sound like a—like *a New York Cat.*"

"*Meoowww,*" the cat loudly replied.

Kaikoa looked up. She was standing by the mango tree.

"I would have called, but I figured the turtles probably told you I was coming." At the sound of her voice, the cat leapt out of Kaikoa's arms.

"Yes. But they didn't tell me right away. That was the longest four weeks I've ever spent."

"2,678,400 seconds of pure torture," she said.

Kaikoa swooped her up in his arms.

He kissed her in a way that meant forever.

"I just have one question," he said as he finally put her feet back on the ground.

"Just one?"

"Well, one really important one."

He went to the old Chinese red cabinet and opened a drawer. He held something behind his back. Her pulse quickened as he knelt down on one knee.

"Will you marry me?"

Her mouth opened but no sound came out. She stared at the exquisite emerald and diamond antique ring and swallowed hard. She wanted to say yes but inane words tumbled out instead. "When? You mean like specifically. Soon?"

"Today. Now."

She nodded her head vigorously. He scooped her up in his arms.

"I take that as a 'yes'.

"Yes! Yes! A thousand times yes!"

He whirled her around as she yelled out the word "Yes" over and over.

The door of the studio burst open. His mother, sister, nieces and nephews and several neighbors stood there. His sister Maile held an antique white lace wedding dress with a long flowing train.

"I knew she'd say yes." Hoku jumped up and down.

"Yay," Keoki cheered. "Now we can eat."

April and everyone else laughed.

His mom approached her, carrying the delicate hand-made dress. "I had to take it in, but I think I got it right," she said. "Mildred helped me."

"Mildred? From the bikini shop?"

"Yes, she'll be there. You can thank her."

"Put it on." Hoku ordered as only a six year old can.

April laughed. "Could I take a shower first?"

"Okay," Hoku said, unable to disguise her impatience.

"These are a gift from Mildred." Maile held up the French white lace bra and panties.

Keoki blushed and Kaikoa playfully covered his eight-year-old eyes. "Hey, those are for my eyes only."

"They have so many holes. I wouldn't want to go swimming in them," Hoku said

Everyone laughed and Hoku laughed with them.

"Everybody's waiting," Kaikoa said sweetly in her ear. He headed for the open door.

"Where are you going?"

"I'll see you down at the beach. Bad luck to see the bride in her dress before the ceremony."

He gave her a sweet kiss that made everyone blush.

* * *

The dress fit perfectly. Kaikoa's sister Maile braided the traditional fragrant white tuberose flowers into April's hair.

"I picked those flowers from the neighbor's garden," Hoku said proudly.

"Thank you. They smell divine. I love them," April said.

"I hope you don't mind that we picked the dress. It was my mom's sister's."

"Honestly, if I had to pick a dress, it would take me a year. This is perfect."

"Mom did a really good job on the alterations. With Mildred's instructions."

April caught a glimpse of herself in the mirror. It took her breath away.

"Okay, you're all done. You look beautiful."

"What do I need to know about a Hawaiian wedding? I mean is there anything special I need to do?"

"Eat a lot."

* * *

The afternoon wedding on the beach was more magical than anything she could have imagined. There were over a hundred people of all ages who had brought colorful tents and beach chairs. Everyone contributed a dish of food, and the array was spectacular. Musicians played and sang, and everyone danced the hula. The ceremony was conducted by an older man, a Hawaiian Kahuna who translated everything into English for her. He helped her with each step as he used the green maile Ti leaf to bind her hands to Kaikoa's, which was a traditional symbol of their commitment to each other. Then he sprinkled water from a large green Ti leaf for the final blessing.

After the ceremony, someone handed her a plate full of food. She only recognized a couple of items—the macaroni salad, fried rice, and the mashed purple Okinawan sweet potato. The rest was mysterious, but definitely from the ocean. She put aside her trepidation because she was hungry. Truthfully, it was all delicious. Nothing compares to homemade food made with love.

Mildred looked over and gave April the shaka hand sign. She whispered loudly to the elder women near her. "You see how the right bikini can change your life?"

"I'm coming in on Monday to get mine," one large woman teased. The others laughed good-naturedly.

Kaikoa's mother had made two three-tiered wedding cakes with lilikoi frosting. It was lighter and more delicious than any cake she had ever eaten.

She and Kaikoa fed each other and licked frosting off each other's fingers.

Later Kaikoa reached for her hand to dance. "They're playing our song."

"Are all these people related to you?"

"One way or another."

The song about the rain finding its way to the sea that he had sung to her that first night at the Bone Yard was played by his band of *cousins*.

He sang it again to her as he danced. It was even more magical now that it was their wedding song.

All the women stopped chatting to watch them, many with happy tears in their eyes.

* * *

The sun was just dipping into the water when he reached for her hand. "Come on, let's slip away."

"But everybody's still here," she said. The crowd had barely thinned. They were mellower, but showed no signs of stopping the eating, drinking, dancing and drumming.

"They'll be here all night. No one expects us to stay."

She let him lead her away, filled with equal parts fear and excitement.

* * *

He led her to a secret cove. He was still wearing the green ti leaf maile lei, the traditional wedding garland that grooms wear during a ceremony. There was a basket waiting there, with a rolled up mat and large, sunset-colored beach towels. She marveled at how prepared he and his whole family were. What if she had gotten the plane the next day, as she had planned? She had a friend from college at the airline who had gotten her a tip that she could leave a day earlier. She made a last minute decision and had flown on standby a day earlier.

How could he have known her arrival date?

It was pointless to ask him how he knew anything. He just always seemed to know.

The full moon rose higher in the sky and the lap of gentle waves was the only sound. He spread out the mat and laid the towels over it. He even had an ice-chest with a bottle of cold champagne.

"Thirsty?" he said, lifting the big bottle.

She hadn't budged from the spot where he had let go of her hand to fix their *bed*.

"You've thought of everything."

"Couldn't possibly do that," he laughed. "Just the essentials." He studied her, smoothly, in no rush.

"Are those your artist's eyes, scrutinizing me?"

"These are my *husband's* eyes. Savoring you."

He took off his lei. Then he slowly unbuttoned his white silk shirt. His bronze skin glistened in the full moon.

She drank in his toned chest and strong arms. She had seen him without a shirt before but now it was *her husband's* bare chest. It was different. More delicious.

He moved behind her and began unfastening the thirty tiny silk-covered buttons on the back of her dress. He took his time. With every slow, reverent opening of a historic button her anticipation rose.

Finally he let the gown slide down to her feet, and she stepped out of its bounds. She wore the demure, white lacy bridal panties and bra that Maile had given her as a gift.

He waited for her to turn and face him. She had never been with a lover who was not rushed or driven to quickly progress to the next stage. As desire coursed through her veins, she wondered if she could be as patient.

With one finger, he traced the curve of her waist and hip, making no effort to remove the thin white lace that was the only barrier left between them.

He unbuttoned his white linen pants. As usual, he wore no underwear. In his fully aroused state, he let his pants slip to the ground.

"I'm all yours." His voice was soft and heavy at the same time.

* * *

Sun streamed in through the old screen doors to the tropical garden outside his bedroom. When she woke up the next morning in his bed the first thing she saw was love in his eyes. How long were you watching me sleep?"

"Just long enough to make sure you were real."

"*Meow.*" Angelina picked her head up to announce her presence and then curled back down between the two dogs, Poi and Taro, at the foot of the bed.

"Guess she likes dogs," he said.

"To say nothing of the fact that she never warms up to strangers."

"I'm not so strange."

"No, you're not strange. You're scary."

"What about me scares you the most?"

"I just never had a dream come true," she said.

Kaikoa pulled the hand-made quilt up higher over her shoulders. "It can be a little chilly in Manoa Valley in the mornings."

"Glad I have you to keep me warm."

"So how does it feel to wake up to a dream come true?"

"I like it," she said. "I'm just scared it's not really real."

"Want me to pinch you?"

"Don't you dare."

Kaikoa pretended to quake in fear at her tone and he accidentally knocked the bedside table. Something fell and he reached down for it. It was her old SWAG watch with grains of sand stuck in the band. He dangled it above her head.

She laughed. "Thanks. But I don't need it anymore."

"Good. Because it doesn't keep time anymore."

"I should send it back to my boss. She told me I was a dreamer."

"In my book that would be a compliment."

"In her book of insults, that's number three."

"Did she fire you?"

"Yes."

"So, we're broke." Kaikoa said it so cheerfully it made her laugh.

"I negotiated a wonderful settlement. Basically, as far as a job, I'm fired. But as a freelancer, I'm hired. I was able to negotiate a higher level of commission—if I can sign up any artists."

"Well, today is your lucky day," he said. "Maybe you will sign one up."

April sat up quickly and the dogs and the cat all jumped. "Did you read the contract?"

"No, the dogs peed on it. But I took that as a positive sign."

"Positive—as in yes? You agree?"

"You probably need at least one client to attract others."

"You're serious, right? You wouldn't joke about this."

"If it means you represent me. And as long as I don't have to read that instant-sleeping-pill of a contract. "

"Of course. And I will re-negotiate that contract," she said, grabbing her tablet from her purse. She made some quick notes. "There are a few issues with the foreign license that you shouldn't give away."

Kaikoa pretended to snore and she punched him playfully.

"Ouch. Isn't that client abuse?"

"Don't give away anything you don't have to. Just sign an agreement on those first three designs that she is out of her mind over: the Mango, the Plumeria, and the Bird of Paradise. I'll get an awesome fee because she has a client drooling over them. We won't show her anything else until the ink is dry." She was excited by the details of the deal.

"Sure." He sat back and watched her. So, while we're waiting for the ink to dry."

He pulled her back down to him.

"Actually, there are a couple more points that I would like to re-negotiate for you," she said. "Now that we are on the same team."

"I figured as much. That's why I knew it was a waste of time to agree to anything before we'd made love."

She grabbed her pillow and walloped him.

Where her pillow had been was a little woven tan *lau hala* box, tied with a red and yellow ribbon. "When did you put this here?

"Hmm, I'd have to estimate, but I'd say approximately 2,678,400 seconds ago. Open it."

April carefully opened the hand-made box. Her jaw dropped. "It's our shell. How did you find it? I so wanted it, but when you told me that story about moving rocks and bad luck . . ."

"After I took you to the airport, I went back and asked the shell to show herself to me if it was supposed to be ours."

April was amazed. The tiny shell was so perfect, so delicate. You could see the light through it when you held it up to the sun. It was full of grace and power and an auspicious symbol of their love.

"You left it under my pillow. What if I had rolled over and crushed it?"

"This shell has traveled thousands of miles, endured hurricanes, and avoided the eyes of tourists. I think she can survive a night under your pillow."

"What are the chances of finding this shell in a whole ocean, then finding it again?" Rather than wait for an answer, April kissed him.

"I couldn't believe my ears, but apparently this shell wants to travel the world," Kaikoa said, shaking his head. "I drew some sketches of the shell. For some reason she wants her image and an inspiring saying to be on your goofy SWAG coffee mugs."

"Oh, my God," April said, pounding the pillow, "I have a great saying and I've been looking for the perfect image for two years."

"Yeah. The shell said you would have it."

"It's never too late to find perfection."

"I like that. I would drink out of that cup."

April's head started to spin. But she looked over at Kaikoa and lay back down. All those ideas would be there tomorrow. This moment was far too precious to let work intrude. She took his hand in hers and kissed every finger.

"So, what do you want to do with the rest of your life?" he asked in a break between kisses.

"Two things."

"And they are?"

"First, make up for four weeks of longing and imagining and thirty years of hoping."

He smiled. "Purrrrfect answer."

He reached for her, pulling away the sheet. "Then what?" he asked?

"Then I want you to teach me how to love in Hawaii Time."

Epilogue

"There is no end. There is no beginning.
There is only the infinite passion of life."

Federico Fellini

About the Author

Genie Joseph was the founder and CEO of Hawaii Movie Studios and is an award winning film and television director. Her feature films have been on Variety's Top 50 list and have won international awards. *SPOOKIES*, a feature film which she co-wrote and directed, is a gothic-horror spoof distributed by SONY. *Spookies* won three awards in the International Festival of Science Fiction and Fantasy Films in Paris. Other feature films such as Alien High and MindBenders have played on USA Cable and other networks.

As a staff producer/director at KITV-4, the ABC affiliate in Honolulu, she directed hundreds of TV commercials. She was also co-producer of Nickelodeon's *Beyond the Break* which shot three seasons in Hawaii. Genie is the author of twenty-one screenplays–eleven of which have been sold and/or produced by independent companies.

She has published several short stories, winning second prize for tasteful erotic fiction in *50 Shades of Natural Gray* by Eve Publishing. She has also been published in various *Chicken Soup for the Soul* books such as *Chicken Soup for the Hawaii Soul*. For seven years has written a *Quality of Life* column for The Honolulu Newspaper. She and Matthew Gray, the Restaurant Reviewer for the Honolulu Advertiser, were co-hosts of LOVE LIFE RADIO—an interview talk radio show in Honolulu for six years. Go to www.Healthy-Relationship-Advice.com for their over 100 articles on communication and love.

Her short films have played at Sundance and many film festivals in the U.S., winning several awards including Best Director at the New York International Independent Film Festival. One of her documentaries called *We Are the PeaceMakers* is an overview of the Peer Mediation Conflict Resolution Program at Leilehua High School. It had a special screening for the Hawaii Judiciary and the Chief Justice, the Honorable Ronald Moon, who greatly praised this video. It is being used to help the Department of education make critical decisions about what programs to support in the future.

With an M.A. in communications, and a Masters in Fine Arts, she teaches Media and Communication at Chaminade University in Honolulu and is a frequent judge at student film festivals. She also taught Television Production and Screenwriting at Olelo, Hawaii's Community Television where she worked with a diverse cross-section of Oahu's multi-ethnic community.

While in New York, Genie had her own production company producing and directing corporate communication and training films. Working with such clients as The New York City Office of Business Development, Chase Manhattan Bank, Jaguar Cars, Mobil Oil, Sports Illustrated, Time, Inc and many other companies.

Currently, she has created a program called *Act Resilient* (www.Act-Resilient.org) which has been presented to over 3,000 US Army Soldiers and their families. *Act Resilient* uses laughter and comedy to help people overcome stress and depression. This program encourages working with animals as part of the healing journey you can see a short film by Genie, *Dogs are Healers,* on You Tube.

To learn more about the ideas in this book, or to order more copies, go to www.GenieJoseph.com/love, or go to Amazon.com.

Genie would love to hear your thoughts about this book. Please email her at Genie@GenieJoseph.com

73711384R00117

Made in the
USA
Middletown, DE